A wish come true . . .

Elizabeth ran into the bathroom. She unlocked the door that led to Jessica's room and burst in—coming face-to-face with the intruder.

"Arrgghhh!" the woman screamed.

But this time, Elizabeth wasn't going to run away. She was going to face the lady down. Slowly, she began to step toward the strange young woman.

The strange young woman seemed to have decided the same thing. She was approaching Elizabeth in the same, slow, cautious manner in which Elizabeth was approaching her.

Their eyes met, and Elizabeth felt another strange sensation. It was the shock of recognition.

She was looking at herself!

Elizabeth saw a flash of images in quick succession. She saw the Christmas carnival. The elf with the chestnut cart. A burst of magical light. A wishing well. Herself making a wish. *I wish I were grown up.* The concentric circles on the water where the coin had penetrated the surface. A sudden, chilly wind.

"Jessica?" she asked in a whisper.

"Elizabeth?" the lady gasped.

As one, Elizabeth and Jessica turned their heads toward the mirror that hung over Jessica's dressing table.

"Arrgghhh!" the

D1367892

SWEET VALLEY TWINS
AND FRIENDS

BIG
for
Christmas

Written by
Jamie Suzanne

Created by
FRANCINE PASCAL

BANTAM BOOKS
NEW YORK · TORONTO · LONDON · SYDNEY · AUCKLAND

RL 4, 008-012

BIG FOR CHRISTMAS
A Bantam Book / December 1994

Sweet Valley High® and Sweet Valley Twins and Friends® are registered trademarks of Francine Pascal

Conceived by Francine Pascal

Produced by Daniel Weiss Associates, Inc.
33 West 17th Street
New York, NY 10011

Cover art by James Mathewuse

ISBN: 0-553-48249-1

Published simultaneously in the United States and Canada

Bantam Books are published by Bantam Books, a division of Bantam Doubleday Dell Publishing Group, Inc. Its trademark, consisting of the words "Bantam Books" and the portrayal of a rooster, is Registered in U.S. Patent and Trademark Office and in other countries. Marca Registrada. Bantam Books, 1540 Broadway, New York, New York 10036.

PRINTED IN THE UNITED STATES OF AMERICA

OPM   0 9 8 7 6 5 4 3 2

To Alice Elizabeth Wenk

One

"I know you're wondering why I called you here today," Janet Howell said to the members of the Unicorn Club, who were seated in her family's living room. She smoothed the hem of the red, green, and gold vest she wore over a short red pleated skirt. There was something very festive and Christmasy about her outfit, and Jessica Wakefield felt a little shiver of holiday anticipation.

"I know you're all exhausted from exams, but I have something very special I want to talk to you about," Janet continued.

Today had been the last day of class before the start of the Christmas vacation. Jessica looked at her watch. It was three thirty. Everybody in the middle school was finished by now.

Jessica looked around the room. All the Unicorns were there. The Howells' Christmas tree was already up and decorated. Red and gold balls hung from each bough, and tiny green and red lights surrounded the tree from its base to its star.

Jessica felt another shiver of Christmas excitement. She loved everything about Christmas. Christmas shopping. Christmas cookies. And Christmas carols.

Most of all, she loved Christmas presents.

There were a lot of presents stacked on the red-velvet Christmas-tree skirt that surrounded the trunk of the Howells' tree. Jessica began to wonder how much she should spend on Janet's gift.

Janet wasn't exactly Jessica's best friend, so she didn't want to spend a fortune on her. But on the other hand, Janet was an eighth-grader and the president of the Unicorn Club, a club made up of the prettiest and most popular girls at Sweet Valley Middle School. That made her an important person, and Jessica wanted to stay on her good side. So it would probably be smart to get Janet a really good present, even though sometimes she was mean and a little snobby to Jessica. Janet sometimes had an attitude about sixth-graders.

Jessica sighed as she watched Janet walking the length of the living room with the air of a runway model.

"She probably called this meeting so she could show off her new outfit," Jessica whispered to Mandy Miller, who sat on the Howells' overstuffed couch next to her.

Mandy covered her mouth, but a giggle escaped anyway. Janet threw an annoyed look in their direction. Jessica put on her innocent-and-very-interested expression.

Janet cleared her throat. "As you all know, the Christmas season has arrived. And I have a holiday treat for all of you."

Jessica leaned forward expectantly.

"My brother, Joe, and I have decided to throw a party in honor of the season. He will be inviting his friends, and I will be inviting mine. Needless to say, all the Unicorns are on my guest list, as well as a few other select individuals from the middle school."

There was a stunned silence as the significance of Janet's speech sank in. Joe Howell was a freshman at Sweet Valley High. If Jessica was understanding Janet correctly, that meant . . .

"You mean your friends and Joe's friends are going to party *together*?" Grace Oliver asked breathlessly.

Betsy Gordon's eyes were wide with surprise. "We're invited to a party with kids from the high school?"

Janet nodded. "That's right."

Lila Fowler, Mandy Miller, and Jessica all clutched at each other's arms and squealed. "All right!"

Tamara Chase and Kimberly Haver jumped up and began dancing and hip-bumping.

Betsy Gordon broke into hiccups, and when Grace Oliver popped out of her seat to join Tamara and Kimberly in their dance, she caused an arrangement of porcelain Wise Men that decorated the coffee table to shake precariously. Betsy dove forward just in time to keep the figurines from toppling.

"Order! Order!" Janet shouted frantically.

But Jessica had to squeal just one more time. She and Mandy both opened their mouths and let out a huge shriek of excitement.

Janet's mouth twitched a little, and Jessica could tell she was trying not to laugh—trying to act like a teacher or something. Janet was like that sometimes.

Jessica joined the other Unicorns as they gave Janet a huge round of applause. Janet might be bossy and snobby, but she was about to include them in the most sophisticated party of all time. After all, not only was Joe a freshman at Sweet Valley High, but he was also on the basketball team. That meant that he would invite his teammates—and some of them were seniors!

Just thinking about the party got Jessica so ex-

cited she could hardly sit still. She jumped up
and high-fived Tamara and Kimberly. Pretty soon
the room was filled with the sound of laughter
and slapping palms.

"Chill out!" Janet commanded in her most
presidential tone.

Immediately, the girls returned to their places.

"Since there will be older men at this party,"
Janet said, "I want to emphasize that it is important that all Unicorns be properly dressed."

"What do you mean?" Mandy asked.

"I mean every Unicorn should do her best to
look mature, sophisticated, and glamorous. No
baby dresses, please. That means no velvet. No
lace. And no bows. I want our club to look hip."
She slowly walked through the living room and
then gracefully pivoted. "Look at what I am
wearing," she instructed.

Jessica cast her eye over Janet's Christmasy en-
semble. Fitted vest. Swingy red miniskirt. A red
leather belt with a gold buckle slung low beneath
the waistband of the skirt. It really was a great-
looking outfit.

Jessica thought about her own wardrobe. Did
she have anything that compared? Janet was not
only older than Jessica, she was bigger, too. That
meant she could shop in the junior and grown-
up departments while Jessica still had to shop in
the girls' department.

Janet stopped in mid-pivot and pointed at Lila. "Now, notice Lila's outfit. Here's an example of another great look."

Jessica saw Lila check her reflection in the mirror over the desk, a little self-satisfied smirk on her face. Jessica couldn't really blame her. After all, if Jessica had been wearing Lila's black denim jeans with a silk shirt and soft leather boots, she would probably have a self-satisfied smirk on her face, too.

Lila was the most fashionable and expensively dressed girl at Sweet Valley Middle School. That was because the Fowlers' housekeeper or chauffeur drove her to Los Angeles once a month to shop. She was able to buy her clothes at the trendiest boutiques and department stores. And she was able to spend as much money as she liked, because her father was one of the richest men in Sweet Valley. Mr. Fowler gave Lila a huge allowance—and spoiled her rotten, as far as Jessica was concerned.

"So let's say we don't get an allowance from Fort Knox," Mandy interrupted. "Then what are we supposed to do?"

Everybody laughed.

"I don't think *you* have to worry, Mandy," Janet told her approvingly.

Jessica knew exactly what Janet meant. Mandy's family didn't have a lot of money, but

Mandy was totally into fashion, and she could put together incredible outfits from thrift stores.

Today she had on a pair of leggings with horizontal red and white stripes that made her legs look like candy canes. Over the leggings, she wore a red chenille V-neck sweater. A black felt hat with a red rose on it sat low on her head. The hat covered her brows and made her large, expressive green eyes look even larger.

Looking around at her friends, Jessica was starting to feel a little uneasy about her own outfit: white jeans and a purple T-shirt with a unicorn on the front. *What was I thinking when I got dressed this morning?* she wondered. *I look like a little kid. And I'm totally out-of-season.* She slumped in her seat. Janet probably wouldn't point to *her* as an example of someone who's well dressed.

"Take a look at Jessica," Janet went on.

Jessica's heart lifted a little. Maybe she didn't look so bad after all. And really, didn't most fashion boil down to force of personality?

Janet looked good in her clothes because she felt superior to everybody.

Lila looked good in her clothes because she was richer than everybody.

Mandy looked good in her clothes because she carried them off with a great sense of humor.

And Jessica looked good in her clothes because . . .

". . . Jessica is a great example of a *fashion don't*," Janet said bluntly as she walked over to Jessica, examining her up and down. "If you're going to wear boot-cut jeans, please wear them with boots, not tennis shoes. And if your T-shirt is faded and practically falling apart, use it to wash the dog or something. Don't wear it to represent the Unicorns. It just makes the rest of us look bad."

Jessica felt a hot flush of indignation rise up the back of her neck. A retort sprang to her lips, but when she looked around the room, she bit her tongue. How could she say anything when she was obviously the worst-dressed person there?

"Don't feel bad," Mandy whispered in Jessica's ear as Janet changed the subject to party decorations. "You always look pretty no matter what you're wearing. That's probably why Janet picked on you. She's jealous."

Jessica managed a smile, but she felt her heart hardening. Janet had no right to treat her like some kind of fashion geek even if she *was* an eighth-grader and president of the Unicorn Club and hostess of a cool Christmas party.

I'll show her, Jessica thought. *I'll look so hot and sophisticated at the Christmas party that Janet'll look like a toddler in comparison.*

Janet was blabbing on and on about how the

right decorations and refreshments were critical for a successful party, but Jessica was hardly paying any attention. Her mind was already focused on the following day, when she would hit the mall and find the most fabulous outfit ever.

"Whew!" Elizabeth Wakefield exclaimed. She opened her locker and began rummaging through the books and sweaters that had collected in there over the last few hectic days. "What a relief to have that over with."

"Tell me about it," said Amy Sutton, her best friend. "I like English and everything, but that exam was really tough."

Elizabeth nodded. "Yeah, it was. But I think I did OK. How about you?"

Amy rearranged a few things in her own locker and then shut the door. "I think I did pretty well. But boy, is my brain tired."

"Mine, too," Elizabeth said with a smile. "I'm ready to shove these textbooks into my locker and forget about them for a couple of weeks."

Her books made a loud clunking noise as she playfully pitched them into her locker. "Stay," she said firmly, holding up her hand, as if she were talking to a dog. Then she quickly shut the locker and pressed her back against it as if she were afraid that the books might actually try to force their way out of her locker.

Amy began to laugh. "I never thought I'd see Elizabeth Wakefield turn her back on books. You're supposed to be the serious and studious twin, remember?"

Elizabeth grinned, thinking about her twin sister, Jessica. On the outside, she and Jessica were absolutely identical. Both girls had long sun-streaked blond hair, blue-green eyes framed by dark lashes, and dimples in their left cheeks.

But their personalities were very different. Jessica loved parties and boys and gossip and being a member of the Unicorn Club. Elizabeth was more serious. She enjoyed reading and writing and serving as the editor-in-chief of the *Sixers*, the Sweet Valley Middle School's official sixth-grade newspaper.

"I'm through being serious and studious for a while," Elizabeth joked. "I'm ready for some fun and excitement this vacation. Oops!" she said, snapping her fingers. "I forgot something." She opened her locker, fished around, and pulled out a book. "It's the latest Amanda Howard mystery. I should return it to the library before it closes for Christmas vacation."

"I didn't know there was a new Amanda Howard mystery out," Amy said eagerly. "Let me see."

"I thought you said your brain was tired," Elizabeth said with a smile.

"My brain is tired from memorizing and study-ing and writing," Amy explained. "But I'm never too tired to read a good book—especially an Amanda Howard mystery."

As Elizabeth handed Amy the book, Amy's face fell. "Darn," she muttered. "I've already read this one."

"I thought *I* was the biggest Amanda Howard fan around," Elizabeth commented with a laugh. "But I think you're ahead of me."

"It was you who got me started," Amy said in a tone of mock accusation. "Now I'm hooked. I can't wait for the new one to come out."

"Well, you *could* always read something else," Elizabeth suggested. "I've read lots of good books lately."

"Like what?" Amy asked.

"*Sadie's Summer in Seattle.*"

"Gag!" Amy groaned. "I can't believe you like that book. It's so childish."

"How about *War in the Kitchen*?"

Amy made a face. "Totally depressing."

"*Zen and the Art of Hopscotch?*"

Amy held up three fingers. "Triple B."

"Triple B?"

"Bland. Boring. Banal."

"Banal?"

"It was on my vocab test. It means ordinary."

Elizabeth laughed and tucked the Amanda

Howard book under her arm. "Come with me to the library, and then we can walk home together."

Amy nodded and fell into step beside Elizabeth. "You know," Amy said with a sigh, "I was really looking forward to this holiday until now."

"What happened to spoil your mood?"

"I realized I'm going to have lots of time off and nothing fun to read. Why is it so hard to find something I like?"

Elizabeth shrugged but smiled a secret smile. Without knowing it, Amy was giving Elizabeth some very helpful hints about what to get her best friend for a Christmas present.

I'll go to the bookstore tomorrow, Elizabeth thought. *They've got thousands of books. I'll find something really wonderful for Amy to read, and I'll give it to her before Christmas so she can start enjoying it.*

"Jessica! Wait up!"

Jessica squeezed the hand brakes on her bicycle and turned around. Elizabeth and Amy Sutton were riding in the street behind her and pedaling hard to catch up.

"It's finally here!" Amy said happily as she and Elizabeth pulled up next to Jessica. "Christmas holiday. Two and a half weeks of fun, food, and presents."

"Don't forget parties," Jessica added with a grin.

"Who's having a party?" Elizabeth and Amy asked at the same time.

"Janet and Joe Howell. On Thursday night," Jessica answered with a grin. It looked as if her serious sister had been bitten by the Christmas bug. Elizabeth's eyes were sparkling with eager anticipation.

"You mean high school kids and middle-school kids together?" Elizabeth asked.

Jessica nodded. "Is that cool or what?"

"Yeah, I guess," Elizabeth said softly. She hesitated. "Though I might feel a little self-conscious around high school kids. Especially the boys."

"No, you won't," Jessica said firmly. "We're both going to look so incredibly glamorous and sophisticated that nobody will know we're only in sixth grade."

"I don't think I have anything glamorous and sophisticated to wear," Elizabeth mused.

"That's because you don't," Jessica said bluntly. "But I'm going to hit Kendall's department store tomorrow and scope out the selections. I'll find something for both of us."

"What about you?" Elizabeth asked Amy. "Do you have anything to wear?"

"I don't think I'll have to worry about that," Amy answered in a resigned tone. "I'm sure I'm not invited."

"Actually, you are," Jessica told her. "I saw the list."

"Really?" Amy said, sounding pleased. "Usually Janet Howell acts like I'm invisible. She totally ignores me."

"Yeah, but Janet will want as many people as possible from school to be there. She doesn't want Joe to outdo her."

Amy and Elizabeth laughed. Over their laughter came a strange sound—a kind of a trumpeting, rumbling, honking sound.

"Did you skip lunch?" Amy asked Elizabeth.

"It wasn't my stomach," Elizabeth insisted.

"It didn't sound like anybody's stomach," Jessica said. "It didn't even sound like anything human."

The trumpeting, rumbling, honking noise sounded again.

"Whatever it is, it's coming from that direction," Amy said, pointing toward Oak Boulevard.

"Come on," Elizabeth urged. "Let's go investigate."

Amy started pedaling along with the twins. "Call me Amanda Howard."

Soon all three girls were riding as fast as they could toward Oak Boulevard. When they turned the corner, Amy and Elizabeth gasped, and for a second Jessica went into shock. "It's an elephant!" she exclaimed excitedly when she got her voice back.

"It's a whole bunch of elephants!" Elizabeth added. "It's a carnival."

"Why are they taking them down Oak Boulevard?" Jessica wondered. "The turnpike would have taken them right to the fairgrounds."

The girls stared as four pachyderms lumbered by, their enormous ears flapping in the breeze. Leading the group was a carnival worker wearing green coveralls. "Had to bring 'em to the fairgrounds this way," he shouted to the girls with a grin. "They wouldn't allow them on your turnpike."

"When does the carnival start?" Amy shouted back.

"Give us two hours," the man replied. "We'll have that carnival up and ready for you kiddies in no time."

Kiddies? Ugh. Jessica hated it when people called her that, and she especially hated it today, after Janet made her feel about two years old. *I can't wait until I'm old enough to be called "Ms.,"* she thought.

"Let's go first thing tomorrow morning," Amy said to the twins.

"Sorry, I can't," Jessica answered quickly. "I'm going shopping tomorrow, remember?" *And besides*, she added to herself, *carnivals are for kiddies*, *not sophisticated middle-schoolers like Elizabeth and me.*

"I've got some shopping, too," Elizabeth said. "But maybe we can go in the evening."

The carnival worker was still smiling and waving. But Jessica tossed her hair haughtily and made a point of not waving back or gawking at the elephants.

She was way too mature for that kiddie stuff!

Two

"Good morning, Steven," Mrs. Wakefield said Tuesday morning at the breakfast table.

Elizabeth almost giggled out loud at the sight of her fourteen-year-old brother. Steven was a freshman at Sweet Valley High and one of the star players on the basketball team. *Well, he may be quick and clear-thinking on the basketball court,* Elizabeth thought, *but right now he looks practically dead.*

Mrs. Wakefield ruffled her son's already ruffled hair affectionately. "Are you awake enough to eat a waffle?"

Steven seemed to brighten a little as he picked up his fork.

"So what's everybody's plan for the day?" Mr. Wakefield asked as he came striding into the kitchen dressed for work.

"Shopping," Jessica and Elizabeth said.

"Sleeping," Steven said at the same time.

"What's your plan for the day?" Elizabeth asked her father.

Mr. Wakefield poured himself a cup of coffee at the counter and then sat down at the table. "Mr. Porter and a few of his associates are in from London for a few days."

Mr. Wakefield was a lawyer, and Mr. Porter was one of his biggest clients.

"Does that mean we won't be seeing much of you until next week?" Mrs. Wakefield asked.

Mr. Wakefield took a sip of juice. "I'll have a lot of meetings today and tomorrow. And then one meeting late Friday afternoon. But after that, I'm free. So I thought Friday night would be a good evening to go get our Christmas tree. Who wants to go pick out the tree?"

"We do," Elizabeth and Jessica said at the same time.

"Steven," Mrs. Wakefield said gently, "what about you?"

Steven responded with an uninterested shrug. "I don't see what you really need me there for."

"Don't you *want* to go?" Mr. Wakefield persisted. "You used to love picking out the Christmas tree."

"Sure," Steven grumbled, "when I was a *kid*."

Elizabeth felt her cheeks grow hot. *It's no big*

deal, she told herself. *Steven's always trying to tease us.*

As she watched him sleepily lift a forkful of waffle to his mouth, she realized Steven wasn't just being a bratty brother. He was too tired and out-of-it to make the effort—which made what he said even worse. It was as though he really thought that only little kids were interested in Christmas trees.

"For your information, Steven, plenty of mature, sophisticated people like Christmas trees," Jessica snapped. "You don't have to be a little kid, you know."

Elizabeth was startled at the defensive note in Jessica's voice. *So Jess is thinking the same thing I am*, she said to herself.

Steven shrugged again. "Whatever," he mumbled, as though he were so far above them, he couldn't even be bothered to respond.

Elizabeth was about to tell him off when she caught the hurt look on her father's face. It made her heart ache.

Every single year, the Wakefields all went to the Christmas-tree lot together and picked out the plumpest, greenest, tallest tree they could find.

Every single year, Mrs. Wakefield insisted that the tree was too big.

That they'd never get it onto the top of the car.

That they'd never get it into the house.

That it was taller than the ceiling.

But every single year, with everybody pushing and shoving and laughing and arguing, they managed to override her objections, get the tree onto the top of the car, and move it into the house.

And every single year, miraculously, the tree stretched up toward the high ceiling of the Wakefield living room, leaving just the right number of inches for the star.

Jessica and Elizabeth always took turns placing the star. Last year it had been Jessica's turn. So this year Mr. Wakefield would lift Elizabeth in the air so that she could place the star on the tree herself.

Elizabeth hated seeing her father looking so unhappy. Obviously, he had been looking forward to their family tradition. And now Steven was acting as if he was too mature for it.

"Please come, Steven," she said.

"Mmm," Steven mumbled into his waffles.

"*Please*, Steven," Elizabeth said, trying to sound coaxing instead of impatient.

Steven looked up. "Huh? Why—" He stopped and glanced around the table. "Well, whatever. I'll go if you really want me to," he said with a dismissive shrug.

"Great!" Mr. Wakefield said in a hearty, happy

voice. "We'll do it Friday evening after I get home from work." He stood, walked over to Mrs. Wakefield, and kissed her cheek. "I'll be home early," he promised. "What about you?"

"No clients this week at all," Mrs. Wakefield answered. She was a part-time interior designer, and her work usually kept her very busy.

"Great," Mr. Wakefield said again. "Then I'll see you all when I get home."

"I'll walk you to the door," Mrs. Wakefield said to him.

As her parents walked toward the door, Elizabeth finished her waffle and watched her brother and sister. Steven's face was practically in his plate, and Jessica looked gloomy.

Finally, Steven broke the silence. "Hey, there's a carnival in town today."

"We know," Jessica and Elizabeth said together.

"Are you going?" Steven asked.

Jessica and Elizabeth exchanged a glance.

"We haven't decided," Jessica said before Elizabeth could answer. "What about you?"

"Who, me? Are you kidding?" Steven asked with a snort. "Those carnivals are for kids. They never even have roller coasters or anything. Just little Ferris wheels and stuff like that. You know—your kind of thing," he added, gesturing toward the twins.

Elizabeth frowned. "What do you mean by that?" she demanded.

Steven raised his eyebrows. "What do you mean, *what do I mean by that*?"

Jessica glared at him. "What do you mean asking her what she means when she says what do you mean by that?"

Steven gave his sisters a confused look. "I'm lost."

Elizabeth took a deep breath. "When you said that *it's our kind of thing*, it was like you were saying we were dumb little kids."

"Yeah!" Jessica put in.

Steven snickered. "Well, exccuuuuuse me. You'd think it was the first time I'd accused you guys of being dumb little kids or something. Since when are you so sensitive?"

"Sensitive?" Jessica asked. "Who's sensitive? The problem here is that *you're insensitive*."

Steven rolled his eyes and began cutting up his waffles again. "Whatever," he mumbled.

Elizabeth was getting tired of his ending conversations this way, as if she and Jessica weren't even worth his attention. "Is that all you're going to say?" she demanded.

Steven looked up wearily. "No, actually. I also want to say that if this is some kind of phase, I hope you two grow out of it soon," he muttered.

*   *   *

Jessica strolled happily through the main floor of Kendall's department store. Christmas was only two weeks away, and the aisles were packed with shoppers.

Jessica loved the Christmas season. Shopping was fun anytime, of course, but it was magical around Christmas. Kendall's was breathtakingly elegant. Tiny, flickering white lights draped from the chandeliers and wrapped around the white columns that supported the high ceiling. Beautiful Christmas accessories filled every counter and overflowed from bins on the floor.

As she reached the hat department, Jessica slowed to browse. The black one with the red plume was incredibly sophisticated. *It'll look amazing with my hair*, she thought, snatching the hat off of the stand. But when she tried it on, the brim settled somewhere around the bridge of her nose.

It was too big. Way too big.

Oh, well, Jessica thought, returning the hat to the display and reaching for another gorgeous one—a forest-green bowler with hollyberry trim.

It practically came down to her chin. Jessica sighed and reached for another hat, an elegant mahogany-colored one.

But it was also too big. Jessica tried on hat after hat. Her head was lost in every single one. *This is crazy*, Jessica thought as she replaced the last hat on the display. *Has anyone ever considered that a twelve-year-old might want to buy a hat?*

"Try the children's department," someone behind her suggested.

Jessica whirled around and saw that the saleslady behind the scarf counter had been watching her.

The saleslady smiled when her eyes met Jessica's. "There's a darling beret up there with a pom-pom on the top. That's what you need, honey." She pointed toward the hat display. "Those hats are for grown ladies."

"Thanks," Jessica muttered, moving quickly away. *And next time mind your own business,* she wanted to say.

A beret with a pom-pom on the top! Get real. Jessica wouldn't be caught dead in a ditch wearing something like that. Babies wore pom-poms.

Jessica fell into step with the crowd of shoppers. She felt listless as the crowd moved her along—as if she were a twig caught in the current of a lake. She hardly even had to move her legs as she drifted past men's ties and wallets, fine jewelry, and handbags.

Suddenly a big sign by one of the makeup counters caught Jessica's eye, and she broke away from the crowd. FREE MAKEOVERS, the sign read. There were high stools by the counters, on which sat mirrors and lavish makeup displays. Jessica moved closer.

"First we'll brush on a little of this shade," a makeup consultant was saying to a plain blond woman sitting on a stool. "It will bring out the red and pink tones in your skin."

Jessica stared in fascination as the makeup consultant proceeded to apply blush, eye shadow, and lipstick to the woman's cheeks, eyelids, and mouth.

As if by magic, the plain blond woman began to look more and more glamorous. *It's amazing,* Jessica thought. *Just a few colors applied the right way, and she's totally transformed.*

Jessica moved a few inches closer. She glanced around the counter and checked the prices on the makeup items. The lipsticks weren't too expensive, but everything else was way out of her price range.

"I'm really not sure I want to buy anything today," the blond woman said a little nervously.

"No problem," the makeup consultant said pleasantly. "You're under no obligation to buy anything. We simply want to familiarize you with our products."

Cool! Jessica thought. *I'll get a makeover myself and then try to find the same shades at the discount pharmacy.*

Jessica moved forward a little more until she

was almost at the elbow of the consultant's white smock.

The makeup consultant bristled and turned around. "Is there something you want?" she asked in an impatient tone.

"I just wanted to get in line for a makeover," Jessica chirped. "Your products look wonderful."

The makeup consultant and the blond woman exchanged a look. The blond woman looked as if she was trying to keep from laughing. The consultant shook her head in irritation. "Little girl, I'm having a very busy day. Now, please go play someplace else."

"But—but I'm not playing," Jessica protested, feeling flustered. "I really want to learn how to use makeup." She cleared her throat and tried to regain her composure. "I mean, I've used it before and everything, but, um, I could use a few hints."

The makeup consultant frowned at Jessica. "Is your mother here with you?"

Jessica shook her head and stepped back a few inches. "No. I came by myself."

"These parents," the consultant hissed at the blond woman. "They treat this mall like it's a day-care center." She turned back to Jessica. "Run along," she snapped.

"But I . . ."

"Soap and water is all you need at your age," the consultant said in a softer tone. She sighed and half smiled as she went back to work on the blond woman. "Why can't little girls understand that they're pretty enough the way nature made them?"

The blond woman smiled. "Odd, isn't it? The young always want to look older. And the old spend a fortune trying to look younger."

Both women laughed. Jessica knew exactly what that laugh meant—it meant they knew something Jessica didn't know, and they weren't going to tell her what it was.

Jessica walked away, her cheeks hot from embarrassment. Why was everyone treating her like a dumb little kid? She wasn't a kid! In a few days she would be going to a party where there would be high school seniors. If those women had known *that*, they would have shown her some respect.

Jessica held up her head importantly as she stepped off the escalator on the third floor. Thinking about the party, she felt her good spirits return. She looked around, dazzled. White-and-gold papier-mâché angels were suspended from the ceiling. And in the center of the floor, there was a huge Christmas tree surrounded by colorfully wrapped boxes.

Jessica began to hum along with the Christmas music as she turned left and headed for the dress department.

*   *   *

"How could you let something like this happen?" Steven groaned to Joe Howell. "You're supposed to be my best friend."

Joe shrugged. "Janet wanted to have a party, and I wanted to have a party. The folks said they couldn't deal with more than one party, so we decided to have it together."

"Don't you see what this means?" Steven said.

Joe frowned. "It means there will be some eighth-graders there."

"Not just eighth-graders, Joe. Seventh-graders, too. And worst of all—sixth-graders. Which means my sisters will be there."

"So what's the big deal? My sister's going to be there, too," Joe answered dismissively.

"Yeah, well, *your* sister is in eighth grade. And there's only one of her. My sisters are in the sixth grade, and there are two of them. They'll probably spend the whole night embarrassing me." Steven sat down on Joe's bed and dropped his head in his hands.

"Oh, come on," Joe argued with a laugh. "How bad could it be?"

Steven shot him a dark look. "I'll tell you how bad. Every time I try to talk to a girl, they'll be standing four steps behind me and giggling. I might as well wear a T-shirt that says DORK." Steven groaned and put his face in his hands again.

"Yeah, I guess I see your point," Joe conceded. "But look on the bright side. Tony Rizzo's sister, who's in sixth grade, will be there, too. All the little kids will probably hang out together and leave us alone. Nobody will even notice your sisters in the crowd."

"Yeah, right," Steven mumbled. "Jessica Wakefield lives to be noticed. And if she *doesn't* get noticed, watch out. There's no telling what kind of crazy thing she'll do to *make* you notice her."

Three

"Horror is very popular right now," the salesman at the bookstore told Elizabeth in an encouraging tone. It was Tuesday afternoon, and Elizabeth was shopping for Amy's Christmas present.

Elizabeth shuddered. "Not with me." She hated horror stories, and so did Amy. "Are you sure you don't have any new Amanda Howard mysteries?"

The salesman shook his head. "Sorry. *The Case of the Missing Ballpoint* is the latest one out."

"She already has that one. Can you recommend anything—besides horror, that is?" Elizabeth asked hopefully.

The salesman scratched his chin. "Sure. There are a lot of other good books just out. There's *Sadie's Summer in Seattle*."

"I don't think so," Elizabeth told him, remembering Amy's reaction. "That book is so childish."

"How about *War in the Kitchen*?"

Elizabeth made a face, just as Amy had done. "Totally depressing."

"Zen and the Art of Hopscotch?"

Elizabeth held up three fingers. "Triple B."

"Triple B?"

"Bland. Boring. Banal."

The salesman tugged ruefully at his ear. "Maybe you should think about getting her something other than a book."

"But that's what she really wants," Elizabeth said. Her eyes swept the shelves again. There were horror books. Ghost stories. Adventure books. There were lots of detective books, but none were as good as the Amanda Howard series.

"How about *King Frog*?" the salesman suggested.

Elizabeth looked at him wearily. "We both read that in third grade."

The salesman shrugged. "I really can't think what else to suggest. Maybe you should try the adult department."

Elizabeth nodded. Maybe he was right. Maybe both she and Amy had outgrown the kids' books.

After all, if they were going to be attending more adult parties, maybe it was time they began reading more adult novels.

*   *   *

Carolyn Farnsworth-Smythe, daughter of an eccentric millionaire in New York, follows her true love west. Along the trail, she meets love, lust, passion, greed, and violence. Can she make her way over the punishing roads that lead the way west? Can she survive the brutalities of man and nature? Will handsome gunslinger William Carlton put down his gun and learn to push a plow? Marion Plotkin's riveting romance will capture your imagination and refuse to let it go.

Elizabeth examined the cover of the thick Western-style romance. On the front, a handsome man and a beautiful woman were locked in a passionate embrace, with the Grand Canyon rising up behind them.

Yuck, Elizabeth thought. The story sounded gross—full of mushy love scenes and gory gunfights. And the jacket was so lurid, Elizabeth was embarrassed to look at it.

If that was what adults read, she'd rather stick with Amanda Howard mysteries. She checked out the signs that hung over the other aisles of the adult section. SELF-vHELP. PHILOSOPHY. TRAVEL. ART. RELIGION. BIOGRAPHIES.

A biography! That was exactly the kind of thing Amy would like. She hurried across the store so quickly that she never saw the saleswoman coming around the corner until they collided.

"Yeow!" the woman cried, dropping an armload of books on the floor.

"Yikes!" Elizabeth shrieked, as one of the books landed on her big toe.

"Are you all right, little girl?" the saleswoman asked, putting her hand on Elizabeth's shoulder and examining her face.

"I'm OK," Elizabeth said quickly. "Are you?"

The woman laughed. "I'm getting used to this. During the Christmas season we have three times as many people in the store as we usually do. And everybody, including me, is in a rush."

She bent over and began picking up the books she had dropped. "As long as I'm here, is there anything I can do to help you?"

"I wanted to buy a book for a friend," Elizabeth told her. "A biography."

The saleswoman pulled a thick book from the pile on the floor. "How about this? It's been on the best-seller list for the last three months. *The Life of Franklin T. Jones: Memoirs of an Industrialist*."

Elizabeth looked at the jacket of the book. On the front cover there was a very formal photograph of an old man wearing a business suit and sitting behind a huge oak desk. "I don't think so," she said. "I'm sure Mr. Jones did a lot of interesting things, but my friend is twelve, like me. She sometimes talks about working in a bank when she grows up, like her uncle, but I don't think she'd want to read a whole book about a businessman."

"OK, then," the woman said as she handed Elizabeth another book. *Vivian Ryan: Up Close and Candid.*

"Who's Vivian Ryan?"

"The most famous actress from the era of silent films."

"Oh," she replied unenthusiastically.

"No? Well, what about . . . *The Life of Churchill?*" She handed Elizabeth an enormous book. "Winston Churchill was a very interesting historical figure. Among other things, he was the prime minister of England during the Second World War."

Elizabeth flipped through the book. It was four hundred twenty pages of small type. *Somehow this doesn't really seem like a vacation kind of book,* she thought as she handed the book back to the woman.

"Well, then," the woman said, "how about—"

"How about that one?" Elizabeth broke in as she spotted a book in the stack with a beautiful picture of a horse on it. *A Pictorial History of the Horse.*

She picked up the elegant book and began examining it. There were glossy pictures of magnificent horses on every page, as well as tons of information about each horse. Elizabeth could imagine Amy absolutely loving a book like this. "I'll take this one," she told the saleswoman.

"Very good," she said with a grin. "Come with me, and I'll check you out."

Elizabeth felt very grown up as she followed the saleswoman to the cash register. And she knew that receiving a beautiful book that came from the adult nonfiction department would make Amy feel very intelligent and adult, too.

She removed her wallet from her purse and waited patiently while the saleswoman gift-wrapped the book in figured silver paper that looked like brocade. Then she tied it with a red bow. When the book was wrapped, the woman placed it inside a glossy green shopping bag with the bookstore's logo discreetly embossed on the paper. Elizabeth took a peek into the bag. The package lay in a nest of green tissue paper and looked like a gift fit for a princess.

As the saleswoman rang up the sale, Elizabeth thought excitedly of how Amy would react to such a beautiful gift.

"That will be sixty-five dollars and forty-two cents," the saleswoman told Elizabeth with a smile.

Elizabeth felt all the air in her lungs whoosh out. *"Sixty-five dollars and forty-two cents? Are you sure?"*

The woman's face fell into a little frown. "Yes, of course I'm sure."

Elizabeth felt herself blush from embarrassment. How could a book cost so much money? Most of the books she and Amy bought didn't even cost ten dollars. "I'm sorry," she said in a mortified voice. "I didn't realize that the book was so expensive. I don't have that much money with me."

The woman smiled indulgently. "I can put the book under the counter here if you'd like to come back tomorrow."

Elizabeth shook her head and felt even more embarrassed. "I won't have the money tomorrow, either," she said softly. "I can't afford a gift that expensive."

The woman leaned over and patted her shoulder. "Don't worry about it. I'll just put this book back on the shelf, and you can look around for something else."

"Thank you," Elizabeth managed to mutter as she walked away.

"What was that all about?" she heard a clerk ask.

The saleswoman who had helped Elizabeth sighed heavily. "A waste of time. Believe me, the next time a little kid tries to buy a book from me, I'm sending them straight to the children's department."

Little kid! Feeling even more mortified, Elizabeth dashed out of the store. Here she was, thinking she was so grown up, and the woman thought she belonged in the children's department. The bookstore had always been one of her favorites, but now she would be too embarrassed to go back there ever again.

The street outside the mall was filled with Christmas street banners and window displays and happy-looking shoppers. All the festivity cheered Elizabeth up a little. *Lots of people make mistakes like the one I made,* she assured herself. *It's no big deal. That saleswoman was just grouchy.*

She took a deep breath and forced herself to stop being angry and embarrassed. When she thought about it, it was really pretty funny. In fact, Jessica and her parents would probably crack up over it that night at dinner.

That will be sixty-five dollars . . . , she thought, remembering the saleswoman's words. She began to laugh herself as she waited at another intersection for the light to turn green. The small group of people who were waiting to cross the street gave her some odd looks, which just made her laugh harder.

By the time she reached her own block, she was convulsed with laughter. She felt too weak to keep walking, so she sat down on the curb while she tried to catch her breath.

"I wish Joe Howell could see this," she heard someone behind her say.

She turned and saw Steven. He was watching her with a mixture of curiosity and horror.

"Hi, Steven," she said through her laughter. "What's new?"

"What's new?" he asked in disbelief. "What's new is that I might as well move out of Sweet Valley and change my name."

Elizabeth's giggles began to die down. "What's the matter with you?"

"Nothing's the matter with me," Steven said gloomily, "except that I'm going to have two sisters at Joe Howell's party that are going to totally embarrass me."

"Embarrass you?" Elizabeth asked. "How could we embarrass you?"

"Well, you're getting off to a good start right now," Steven snapped. "Sitting here on the curb by yourself and laughing like a hyena." His eyes darted around, from one house to another. "The neighbors probably think you're drunk or something."

That did it. Elizabeth's mouth went dry, and she felt nothing but fury. "Steven Wakefield!" she yelled. "You apologize right now."

"For what? Being more mature?"

"Oh, right," she said sarcastically. "I forgot you were the mature one in the family. Too bad you weren't mature enough not to hurt Dad's feelings this morning when you acted like you didn't care about our Christmas tree."

"I did *not* hurt his feelings," Steven protested.

"You did too," Elizabeth insisted.

"Look," Steven said angrily. "You're twelve. Remember? That means you don't know as much as I know about anything—and that includes Mom and Dad."

"Do me a favor," she said. "Quit bragging about being fourteen when you act about ten."

"Do me a favor," he countered. "Don't come to Joe's party. Please. I'll do your chores for two weeks."

Elizabeth felt a stab in her stomach. She had been really excited about the party, and it hurt her feelings that Steven didn't want her there. But she wasn't about to let Steven know how upset she was. "It's Janet's party, too, you know," she said stiffly.

"Don't remind me," Steven groaned. "It's bad enough that I'll probably have Janet hanging around me all evening. Add you and Jessica, and it's like I'll be baby-sitting all night." He turned and began to walk away, his shoulders slumped.

Elizabeth stared after him. Finally, she threw her purse down and cupped her hands around her mouth like a megaphone. *"And a very merry Christmas to you too!"* she yelled sarcastically.

Four

Velvet. Lace. Bows.

Jessica flipped through the racks in Kendall's dress department with a growing sense of frustration.

"That's cute," a woman commented as Jessica removed a dress from the rack and examined it.

Jessica immediately replaced the dress. "Cute" was definitely the kiss of death among the Unicorns. Elizabeth wore clothes that were cute—and sweet and understated and little-girlish.

Jessica loved Elizabeth, but *sheesh*. She was always dying to empty out the contents of Elizabeth's closet and burn them. All those blouses with the Peter Pan collars. And Elizabeth still wore socks with her party dresses!

That reminded Jessica that she needed to try to

find a dress for Elizabeth to wear to the party. She should probably try to advise Amy on the dress code, too. With their babyish clothes, those two could really embarrass her *and* make Janet look bad—which wouldn't be too great for Jessica's standing as a Unicorn.

She pulled another dress from the rack. It was sort of a silky purple material with a small floral print. *Purple—perfect*, Jessica thought. The Unicorn Club's official color was purple, the color of royalty. The Unicorns all tried to wear something purple every day, particularly on special occasions.

She turned the dress around to see the back. *Ick*, she thought with disappointment. It had a sash that tied in a great big baby bow. She returned the dress to the rack.

"Are you looking for something in particular?" a saleswoman asked, approaching her from behind.

Jessica nodded. "A party dress."

"Well, as you can see, we have a lot of those," the woman said with a laugh.

"Yes, but these aren't exactly what I had in mind," Jessica said, trying to sound adult.

The woman frowned. "I don't know what you mean."

"I need something a little more . . . sophisticated. Everything I've seen has a lace collar or a bow or a sash." She stood a little straighter. "I'm going to a party with some kids from high school."

The saleswoman smiled. "Then you do need a special dress," she agreed. "How about this one?"

The woman quickly flipped through the dresses and pulled out a bright-red dress with a black patent leather belt. "This ought to fit you."

Jessica studied the dress. It was kind of plain, but at least it didn't have a lace collar or a bow in back. "I'll try it on," she said.

The saleswoman led her into the dressing room.

Inside her cubicle, Jessica pulled off her jeans and purple T-shirt. She took the red dress off the hanger, pulled it on over her head, and struggled with the zipper in the back.

After a few moments of reaching and tugging, she managed to get it zipped. Then she cinched the black patent belt around her small waist. *So far so good*, she thought. It felt as if the dress fit perfectly. Jessica walked out of the dressing room toward the full-length mirror on the other side of the dress department.

When she reached the mirror, she sighed happily. The dress was great. And the color made it perfect for a Christmas party. All she would need were some low-heeled black patent leather shoes and—

"Look, Mommy," she heard a young-sounding voice say. "That little girl's dressed just like me."

Jessica whirled around, and her jaw dropped. A little girl who looked about nine years old had on the exact same dress. And it looked just right on her.

The saleslady appeared again. "What do you think?" she asked.

"I think I need to look some more," Jessica responded gloomily. *Like in another store,* she added to herself.

Back inside the cubicle, she hung up the dress and began putting her own clothes back on. Just as she finished dressing, there was a little knock on the door. "I can take back the dress," the saleswoman called.

Jessica opened the door. "Here you go," she said, handing the saleswoman the dress. "Thanks for your help."

"Actually," the saleswoman said, "I had an idea. Why don't you try our new petite department? They would have more sophisticated clothes in small sizes."

Jessica's heart lifted. "That's a great idea," she said happily.

"It's on the second floor," the saleswoman said.

"Thanks!" Jessica said as she hurried away. "Thanks a lot! Oh—and merry Christmas."

The saleswoman smiled. "Thank you. Merry Christmas to you, too. And merry Christmas party."

Jessica stood in the petite department dressing room and eagerly pulled the first dress off the hanger.

Coming to the petite department had been a wonderful, fabulous, unbelievably terrific idea.

There were lots of clothes in this department that she liked, and Jessica had taken five dresses into the dressing room to try on.

She stepped into a sleeveless black sheath dress with a giant tiger head stitched onto the front. It was the coolest dress she had ever seen.

The sheath dress slipped easily past her shoulders.

Too easily. Jessica felt as if she were wearing a big sack.

She lifted her arms. Bad move. The armholes were so big, someone could practically look through one and see past her chest through the armhole on the other side.

She tried holding the dress by the shoulders. Maybe with a little alteration here and—

"Oh, dear, that's way to big for you." The

petite-department saleswoman was peering over the cubicle door at her.

"Yeah, I guess it is," Jessica admitted with a sigh, as she dropped the shoulders. "Do you have a smaller size?"

The saleswoman shook her head. "Everything you've got in there is the smallest size we have. I'm afraid all of it is going to be too big."

Jessica let out another long and disappointed sigh. "Can you suggest someplace else I should look?"

The saleswoman studied Jessica's slim figure. "Why don't you try the first-floor girls' department?" she suggested.

"... so then I yelled *'and a very merry Christmas to you, too,'*" Elizabeth told Jessica on Tuesday evening.

Jessica sat on the end of Elizabeth's bed, waiting for her sister to finish her little tirade. She had to admit that for once in her life, Jessica didn't exactly blame Steven. After all, he probably felt the same way Jessica was feeling about Elizabeth and Amy. They didn't have to do anything major to embarrass her. Just showing up in their dweeby baby clothes would be enough to make Jessica look bad.

"Well?" Elizabeth sputtered after a few moments had passed. "Don't you have anything to say? Are you just going to sit there like a lump?"

Jessica jumped at Elizabeth's sharp tone. *Sheesh*, she thought. *Steven's really gotten under her skin.*

"Say something," Elizabeth commanded.

Jessica bit her lip and pretended to be examining her nails. *Sorry, Lizzie, but I know how he feels about this one*, she thought.

"What do you mean, you know how he feels about this one?" Elizabeth shouted.

Jessica jumped again. She hadn't meant to say it out loud. Elizabeth plopped down in her desk chair and gave Jessica a tired, hurt look. "Jess, what's with you?"

Jessica took a deep breath. "Well, what I mean is, he doesn't want us to go to the party and look like babies."

Elizabeth blinked in confusion. "Why would we look like babies?"

"Because all we have are baby dresses," Jessica answered in disgust. She stood up and began to pace. "I scoured Kendall's this afternoon, looking for dresses for both of us, and I couldn't find a thing."

"Then I think I'll wear my blue dress with the . . ."

". . . bow in the back?" Jessica finished for her.

"Yes. It's my . . ."

". . . favorite?" Jessica finished for her.

Elizabeth nodded.

"Listen, Elizabeth, that's exactly the kind of thing that would give us a bad name. It's a drip dress," Jessica said matter-of-factly.

"It is *not* a drip dress," Elizabeth retorted.

"It is too a drip dress."

"Are you calling me a drip?"

"No, I'm calling your blue dress with the bow in the back a drip dress. You've got a closet full of dork togs, and I don't want you to show up at the coolest party of the whole year in a triple-D dress."

"A triple-D dress?"

"Drippy. Dorky. Dweeby," Jessica explained, crossing her arms over her chest.

Elizabeth looked down at her hands, a frown creasing her forehead.

Normally, Jessica felt bad when Elizabeth's feelings were hurt, but now she was too irritated to care. It didn't even matter if her sister felt like murdering her. The truth had to come out. It was time Elizabeth faced up to some fashion facts.

Elizabeth finally looked up. "You're right," she admitted in a reluctant tone.

Jessica's looked at her sister suspiciously. Having Elizabeth admit that Jessica was right and she was wrong was unusual enough. But over the issue of clothes, it was completely un-precedented.

"I know, I know," Elizabeth continued. "I don't usually let you talk me into dressing a certain way, but considering there *will* be high school seniors at this party . . ."

"You'll actually look as I command you to?" Jessica finished hopefully.

Elizabeth rolled her eyes. "Yeah, I guess I could try obeying your fashion commands, Master Jessica. After all, it's for the sake of looking more mature. So tell me what to do."

Jessica's brows settled back into a frown. "Unfortunately, that's the problem. I mean, I could help you dress for school every day, but Sweet Valley just doesn't have any sophisticated party clothes for kids our age."

There was the faint sound of a phone ringing, and then Jessica heard her mother calling her from downstairs. "Jessica. Phone."

Jessica stood. "Wait here. I'll be back."

As she ran out the door, she noticed Elizabeth staring gloomily into her closet.

"Dorky!" Elizabeth exclaimed, pushing her pink velvet jumper across the bar of her closet. The metal head of the hanger made a loud rattling noise as it slid along the steel rod.

"Dweeby!" she groaned, examining her soft paisley-printed cotton-and-lace dress.

"Drip, drip, drip, drip, drip," she repeated as

she sent her dresses, one by one, rattling across the bar to the other end of the closet.

Jessica was right. Her clothes were babyish.

The next time a little kid tries tries to buy a book from me, I'm sending them straight to the children's department.

The bookstore clerk's remark echoed over and over in Elizabeth's head. After Steven's implication that she acted as if she were a little kid and Jessica's comment that she *looked* like a little kid, Elizabeth didn't think the remark was so funny anymore. In fact, the thought of it made her feel sick and ashamed. It made her wish she could walk into that store like a grown-up—wearing chic, adult clothes—and buy *three* books from the adult section.

I'd rather die than go to that party in any of these dresses, she thought. She could feel tears welling up in her eyes. She blinked and brushed them away. *What's going on with me?* she wondered. *I can't believe I'm about to start bawling because I don't have anything to wear.* "It's like I'm becoming Jessica or something," she muttered.

"It's like you're becoming me?" Jessica asked, bouncing into Elizabeth's room. "Why would—" She broke off when she saw Elizabeth's face. "Chill!" she ordered.

Elizabeth bit her trembling lip.

"Seriously, Lizzie, our problems are over," Jessica announced happily.

"Don't tell me," Elizabeth quipped in a hoarse voice. "You're going to take a class in speed sewing and run us up a couple of double-D dresses."

"Double-D?"

"Drop-dead dresses," Elizabeth explained.

Jessica grinned. "Better than that. The Fowlers' chauffeur is going to drive Lila into Los Angeles tomorrow to shop, and I'm invited to come along—which means I'll definitely find something cool for us to wear."

"Isn't there one little problem? You can't afford to shop where Lila shops, remember?" Elizabeth pointed out.

"No prob," Jessica assured her. "While Lila's shopping at the pricey boutiques, the chauffeur can take me to the outlet mall."

Elizabeth gave Jessica a quick hug. "Even though I still think you're way too hung up on fashion, I'm really glad you brought this up. I mean, I don't want to show up at the party looking like a fourth-grader. Thanks for helping me."

"Are you kidding? I'm glad you're finally taking my fabulous fashion advice," Jessica said, smoothing her hair. "Hey, don't roll your eyes at me."

"OK," Elizabeth said, rolling her eyes.

"Oh, by the way," Jessica continued, blushing

a little, "the Unicorns are all going to the carnival tonight. Want to come?"

"I thought . . ."

"Yeah, I know. But if an eighth-grader like Janet Howell wants to go, how babyish could it be?"

Five

"Steven was way wrong about this place," Jessica whispered to Elizabeth at the carnival. "It's totally cool."

Elizabeth smiled. "I'm glad we came. Everything is so beautiful."

The Christmas carnival looked like Christmas in fairyland. Elizabeth couldn't figure out how they did it, but somehow the carnival managed to seem cold, snowy, and Christmaslike even though they were in the middle of California.

The carnival color scheme was white and gold with red and green flecks. The night air had the hint of a sharp chill in it. And when Elizabeth heard the jingle of the harness bells on the ponies, she got a warm, happy feeling in the pit of her stomach.

She recognized that feeling. It was the Christmas spirit. And she never knew from year to year when exactly she was going to catch it. Sometimes the first whiff of pine in the Christmas-tree lot would jump-start her Christmas spirit. And sometimes it was the smell of gingerbread coming from the Wakefield kitchen that kindled her excitement.

But this year, Elizabeth thought it was the happy look on her sister's face as they walked past the booths, with their glittering lights and shimmering tinsel. Usually, when Jessica was around the other Unicorns she affected a cool and aloof attitude, but this evening her face was open and glowing.

Elizabeth was even enjoying being around the other members of the Unicorn Club. None of them were acting the least bit mean or snobby.

"Look," Jessica said, pointing. "Hot chestnuts."

Elizabeth saw a little man dressed like an elf standing beside a pushcart. The pushcart was little more than a metal bin placed over a coal fire on wheels. The elf stood beside it, wearing woolen mittens and poking the fire with a pair of tongs.

"Let's get some," Jessica said excitedly. "I've never actually eaten any roasted chestnuts."

"Neither have I," Elizabeth added.

"Come on, you guys," Mandy urged. "We can get chestnuts later. If we don't hurry up and get in line, we'll miss the merry-go-round."

"You guys go on ahead and get us a place in line," Jessica said. "Elizabeth and I will catch up with you in a couple of minutes."

The other Unicorns hurried off in the direction of the rides. In the distance, Elizabeth could hear the pipe organ inside the merry-go-round cranking out familiar Christmas tunes.

The night breeze ruffled past her, lifting the stray tendrils of blond hair that surrounded her face. She shivered a bit and turned up the jacket of her coat as Jessica hurried toward the chestnut stand.

The breeze ruffled past her ear again, carrying Jessica's voice. "Come on, Elizabeth. Hurry!"

Elizabeth ran to catch up with her sister, and as she neared the chestnut cart, she got a closer look at the elfin vendor. He wore green leggings and a green shirt with a red vest. He also wore a floppy stocking cap and little green shoes that curled up at the toes.

"Good evening, ladies," the man said. His face was old and weather-beaten, but it was so rosy-cheeked and merry, Elizabeth couldn't stop staring. He looked as though he had come straight from Santa's workshop.

"May I have some chestnuts, please?" Jessica asked.

"Yes, ma'am," the chestnut vendor said politely.

Elizabeth noticed that Jessica stood a little taller. The man was treating them like grown-ups—saying "ma'am" and calling them "ladies."

As though he had suddenly become aware of Elizabeth's stare, the vendor turned his head slightly. When his eyes met hers, there was a flash of light so bright, and so white, that it was as if someone had taken a picture with a flashbulb.

Elizabeth blinked and looked over at Jessica, who was busy counting out change for a little paper bag full of chestnuts. She didn't seem to have noticed the flash of light at all.

The man put all but one quarter into his pocket. He tossed the quarter into the air and caught it with an elaborate flick of his wrist. Another deft motion of his hand sent the coin sailing over his shoulder.

There was a soft plinking sound.

That was when Elizabeth noticed that behind the chestnut stand there was a well—a Christmas wishing well decorated with pine boughs and red berries.

"I'm making a Christmas wish," the vendor

said with a smile. "I'm wishing the two of you an unforgettable Christmas."

Elizabeth smiled back. "Thank you. I hope your Christmas is a happy one, too."

"Happy and unforgettable aren't always the same thing," he answered with an enigmatic smile. Then he pulled on the handles of his cart and began wheeling it away and into the crowd. "Chestnuts!" he cried. "Hot chestnuts!"

What a strange thing to say, Elizabeth thought. But before she could think about it much longer, she felt Jessica clutch her arm.

"Elizabeth!" Jessica hissed. "Look."

Jessica pulled Elizabeth several feet away and nodded in the direction of the snow-cone stand.

"It's Steven," Elizabeth said in surprise. "I guess he doesn't think Christmas carnivals are so babyish after all!"

"Let's go over and tease him!" Jessica said urgently.

She began to plunge forward, but Elizabeth grabbed the back of her purple sweatshirt and pulled her back.

"Hey, what's the deal?" Jessica asked. "This is the perfect chance to get back at him. And by the way, let go of my sweatshirt."

Elizabeth loosened her grip. "Listen, Jess, if we tease him now, won't that kind of just prove his point? I mean, he's already worried we're going to embarrass him at the party."

"Hmmm, good point," Jessica said thoughtfully. "So let's go over and blow him away by *not* embarrassing him."

Not a bad idea, Elizabeth thought as she followed her twin. But as they got closer, Elizabeth began to get a better sense of why Jessica was so excited to speak to their brother. Standing next to Steven and Joe Howell was another boy—someone she'd never seen before. All she knew was that he was really, really handsome.

"Hi, Steven," Jessica called out. Elizabeth smothered a giggle. Jessica was using her *grownup* voice. It sounded like Janet Howell with a little dash of Lila Fowler thrown in. And she usually reserved it for when she wanted to impress a guy.

"Hello, Jessica," Steven responded, mimicking her theatrical voice. Elizabeth bristled. When Steven spoke that way, it wasn't at all funny.

Jessica shot Steven a dark look. "I thought you said Christmas carnivals were for babies."

Steven paled a little. "Which explains what you two are doing here," he retorted.

Jessica's cheeks reddened again, and Elizabeth felt sorry for her sister and angry at Steven at the same time. "We just wanted to say hello," she told him in a clipped tone.

"Hello and good-bye," Steven said, starting to turn away.

"Wait a minute, Steven," the cute boy said. "You haven't introduced me to your sisters yet." He gave Elizabeth and Jessica a warm smile. "It's pretty amazing how you two look exactly alike."

Steven sighed. "Tim Reed, meet my sisters, Elizabeth and Jessica," he said in a bored tone.

"Pretty names," Tim said with a smile.

"Thank you," Jessica said in her mature voice.

"Hey," Tim said, leaning closer, as though he were telling the twins a secret, "I'll bet you guys have played some great tricks on Steven, haven't you?"

Steven groaned dramatically.

Tim laughed. "That answers my question."

Elizabeth and Jessica began to laugh, too.

"Tell me the best trick you ever played."

"*Well*," Jessica said, putting a finger to her lips. "There was the time we tricked some con artists who were trying to rob everybody in our neighborhood. Of course, we fooled a lot of people besides Steven then."

"Sounds like quite a trick—like an Amanda Howard mystery or something," Tim said.

"You like Amanda Howard mysteries?" Elizabeth asked excitedly.

"Definitely," Tim said. "My aunt's an editor in

New York, and she edits the Amanda Howard books."

Elizabeth was so impressed, she could hardly speak. "That's the kind of thing I'd love to do when I grow up," she said.

"Really?" he asked, looking at her intently. "Me, too. I love any kind of mystery and I especially love mysteries that have teenage detectives. Now, tell me about the Elizabeth and Jessica Wakefield mystery."

Steven screwed up his face. "Come on and I'll tell it to you over by the dart game. It'll take forever if they tell you."

"Jessica!" They heard a faint cry. "Elizabeth! Come on. It's our turn."

"We'd better go," Elizabeth said reluctantly. "Our friends are waiting for us at the merry-go-round."

"Not that we make a habit of riding merry-go-rounds," Jessica said in her grown-up voice.

"I think it's a great thing to make a habit of," Tim said. "Mind if I come with you?"

"Mind?" Jessica asked breathlessly. Then she cleared her throat. "That is, not at all. We'd love to have you come with us. Would you like a chestnut?"

Tim reached into Jessica's bag as Steven let out another groan.

Elizabeth pressed her lips together so she

wouldn't grin. *Too bad, Steven,* she thought, *but your friend seems more interested in me and Jessica than he does in you.*

"Now you've done it," Steven said darkly.

"Done what?" Tim asked.

"Riding the merry-go-round with them. Laughing at their jokes. Meeting all their little friends. Telling Elizabeth that she could write to your aunt in New York. Telling Jessica to save the first dance for you. You know what's going to happen, don't you? They're going to stick to you like glue at the party," Steven said. "I just thought you should be warned."

"I'm not too worried about that," Tim said calmly. "They seem like nice girls. It must be pretty cool to have twin sisters."

"Not exactly," Steven said sullenly.

"Hey, man, why are you so uptight about them?" Tim asked.

Steven shrugged and frowned. It was hard to explain why he was especially uptight about Elizabeth and Jessica right now. After all, even though he teased his sisters a lot, he really thought they were pretty great kids.

Kids! That was it. It was totally irritating to have two shrimpy brats hanging around and embarrassing him all the time—especially at a party where there would be a lot of pretty girls and a lot of guys from his basketball team. And a bunch of those guys would be seniors.

He hadn't been to many parties with high school seniors. What if he said or did something dumb and ended up seeming like a total dweeb?

But, of course, he couldn't let on that he was worried about that.

Not to Joe.

And not to Tim.

And especially not to his sisters.

He was the oldest. He was in high school. He was supposed to be cool.

Even if he didn't feel cool at all.

Even if he felt like a kid himself.

"I can't believe how lucky you are, Jessica," Betsy Gordon said with an envious sigh. "Tim Reed wants to dance with you at the party."

Jessica's heart was still pounding. Tim had followed the girls to the merry-go-round, met all her friends, and then ridden along with them three times in a row. *Three times!* she thought dreamily.

He'd been incredibly nice. He had talked a long time to Elizabeth about how they both wanted to try writing mystery novels.

But as flattered by the attention as Elizabeth was, Jessica knew that Tim paid *her* the highest compliment of them all—he had asked her to save the first dance for him at Janet's party.

Jessica reflected on the moment when he had asked that magical question, but the details were a little foggy. Someone had said something about the band. Then Tim had said something. When Jessica had turned her head to face him, she had caught a glimpse of the Christmas elf as he pushed his chestnut cart through the crowd of people surrounding the carousel.

For a second, her eyes had met the elf's. And it had given Jessica the oddest sensation. She had seen a sudden explosion of bright light. At first she had thought it was a flashbulb.

But when her eyes had adjusted, she had looked all around and hadn't seen anyone with a camera. She had been so busy trying to figure out what had happened that she hadn't even realized Tim had been talking to her until he tapped her shoulder. "I'm sorry," she had stuttered. "What did you say?" Tim had smiled and then repeated his question. *"Will you save the first dance for me?"* She sighed at the memory.

"So, Jess, what are you going to wear to the party?" Mandy asked, bringing Jessica's mind back to the present.

"Don't worry," Jessica said with an airy wave of her hand. "Lila and I are going shopping in Los Angeles tomorrow."

"I'm very pleased to hear that, Jessica," Janet

Howell said with a sniff. "This is *the* party of the year. And even though you and Elizabeth are only in the sixth grade, you have a responsibility to the rest of us to try to fit in with the older guests."

Jessica tossed her hair haughtily. She remembered what Mandy said about Janet feeling jealous of her for looking good no matter what she wore. And now she was probably jealous of her and Elizabeth because they had been the ones to bring a cute high school boy over to the merry-go-round. They had been the ones he had talked to the most. And they were the ones he would be looking forward to seeing on the night of the party.

Janet hadn't had the same luck with the high school guy whom *she* had a big crush on— Steven. When Steven and Joe had joined Tim and the girls at the merry-go-round, Janet had dropped a lot of hints about wanting to dance with him. But Steven hadn't paid any attention at all.

He had just stood on the edge of the carousel, staring dismally out into the night.

"Come on, Steven," Joe called.

Steven quickly reached into his pocket for some change to buy chestnuts from the little man dressed like an elf. Steven wasn't actually sure why he was buying chestnuts. It just seemed like a Christmasy thing to do.

Steven was glad Joe and Tim had wanted to come to the carnival. He would never have had the nerve to suggest doing something that sounded so babyish. But now he could just act as if he were along for the ride—it wouldn't seem as if he got a kick out of this kiddie stuff or anything.

As it turned out, he really wasn't having a good time anyway. This business about Jessica and Elizabeth was really bugging him. It seemed as though every time he turned around, Jessica had developed a crush on one of his friends and then come up with one crazy, complicated plan after another to attract the friend's attention.

Why couldn't she and Elizabeth leave his friends alone and hang out with kids their own age? Why did they think they could do everything he did? He was the oldest, and they were just twelve.

"Here's your change, sir."

Steven quickly looked around. Was the elf talking to a man in back of him? But there was no one around.

"Sir?" the vendor repeated.

That's when Steven realized that the elflike guy was talking to him—calling him "sir," as if he were an adult. Steven stood up tall. "Thank you," he said in a firm, businesslike tone.

The elf smiled. As Steven turned away, his eyes met the vendor's for a split second. And for only a second, a star-shaped flash of light burst in front of Steven's eyes.

Six

"Where did you get all that stuff?" Elizabeth asked incredulously late Wednesday afternoon. "And what is it?"

"Jackets. Trousers. Skirts. And accessories," Jessica explained with a grin as she emptied another bag of stuff onto Elizabeth's bed.

Elizabeth smiled. She hated to admit it, but she was looking forward to going to the Howells' party the next night as much as Jessica—and she was just as eager to see Tim again as Jessica was. He had been really fun to talk to.

Elizabeth had never met a boy who had read Amanda Howard mysteries before. And he had told her that he'd love to talk with her about the kind of books they hoped to write or edit when they grew up.

"So what do you think of this stuff?" Jessica asked, upending another bag.

Elizabeth began to examine the things Jessica had strewn across the bed. Beaded purses. Glittering bracelets. Feather collars. Tiny jackets in beautiful colors and designs.

Some of the garments were studded with stones, and some of them were covered in sequins. There were small silk trousers in beautiful colors, and tiny evening sandals.

"How could you afford all this?" Elizabeth marveled. Then she was hit with a horrible thought. "Jess! You didn't sneak out with Mom's credit card, did you?"

Jessica flicked a chiffon scarf at Elizabeth's face. "Of course not."

Elizabeth blew the gauzy scarf out of her face. "Then how did you pay for all this?"

"I told you about the discount mall in L.A., right? Well, after the chauffeur dropped Lila at Theodore's Boutique, he drove me there." Jessica scrunched up her face in distaste. "Yuck. You can't believe the stuff they had for people our age. It was worse than Kendall's."

"Well, this stuff definitely isn't yucky," Elizabeth said, picking up a soft cashmere sweater with tiny rhinestones sprinkled along the sleeves. The sweater was a beautiful emerald green. With the matching silky green skirt, it would look perfect for the Christmas party.

"Yeah, well, we were driving back to the main shopping district to meet Lila when I saw this sign that said 'garage sale,'" Jessica continued.

"You got this stuff at a garage sale?" Elizabeth exclaimed.

"Can you believe it? The lady who was having the sale was really small—just about our size. And she sort of looked like a teeny-weeny Mrs. Santa Claus. Red cheeks and white hair."

"And these were her clothes?"

Jessica nodded. "She said she had always loved beautiful clothes but had never been able to find any that were small enough. So she designed and sewed the clothes for herself. She used to be a dancer and singer at the Christmas carnival. But after she retired, she never had any place to wear them. So she decided to sell them."

"How incredibly lucky," Elizabeth said a little breathlessly. She liked picturing the teeny-weeny Mrs. Santa Claus. But somehow these clothes didn't look like the kind of clothes a Mrs. Santa Claus–type lady would wear.

For that matter, they didn't look like the kind of clothes Elizabeth Wakefield would normally wear either. She couldn't wait to start trying things on. She wanted to look grown up and sophisticated—just like a New York writer—when she saw Tim Reed at the party.

She smiled to herself. *I'm really starting to get carried away with this Tim Reed stuff. If I don't watch myself I'll start seeming as boy-crazy as Jessica.* She looked at her sister to bring herself back down to earth. "So what did Lila think of our new clothes?"

Jessica shrugged. "Beats me. Lila didn't want to look at them. She said shabby old clothes depress her."

Elizabeth groaned. "I know Lila's your best friend and everything, Jess, but she's probably also the biggest snob in Sweet Valley. These clothes are totally beautiful. They're not old or shabby at all."

Jessica smirked. "Yeah, well, Lila will have to find that out for herself at the party. And when she sees us she's going to be green with envy. Because I did happen to see the dress she got at Theodore's. And guess what?"

"Hmmmm. It's velvet with a lace collar?" Elizabeth ventured.

"And a bow in back," Jessica added with a laugh. "She said it was all she could find in her size on such short notice. She pretended like she thought it was something great, but I know Janet will freak when she sees it. So it looks like *we* are going to have on cooler clothes than anybody else. *We* are going to look totally grown up and Lila is going to look like a total loser."

Elizabeth watched her sister throw a glittery scarf joyfully in the air and sighed. "I have to say, Jess, I don't feel too great about the idea of getting dressed up just to make other people feel bad."

"Who's trying to make anyone feel bad?" Jessica asked innocently. "I just want to make a few people—Janet and Lila, to be specific—eat their words. You know, show them what good fashion sense is all about. Don't you want to rub anyone's face in how cool you'll look?"

"Hmmm. Now that you mention it, I do," Elizabeth said, pretending to look thoughtful. "You, to be specific."

"Ha! Ha!" Jessica responded dryly.

Actually, there's someone else I'd like to see eat a few words, Elizabeth thought as she watched Jessica pick up a silky skirt with a fluted hem and twirl in front of the mirror. Steven's words replayed in her head.

Do me a favor. Don't come to Joe's party. Please.

I'll do your chores for two weeks.

Add you and Jessica and it's like I'll be baby-sitting all night.

Well, nobody would think he was there to baby-sit his sisters when his sisters looked almost as old as he did—and maybe even older. Elizabeth stood next to Jessica in the mirror. "So, Jess, will you make up my eyes tomorrow night?" she asked.

Jessica raised her eyebrows. "You—my pure, natural sister—wearing eye makeup?" She put her hand on her forehead, as if she were feeling faint.

"I'm wearing makeup, all right," Elizabeth confirmed with a tiny smile. "And lots of it."

"We'll take six of those chocolate pastries," Mr. Wakefield said, trailing his finger along the glass case in the bakery section of the grocery store. "And how about an assortment of those cookies. Two dozen ought to do it."

"Yes, sir," the clerk said with a smile.

Steven squirmed impatiently. It was late Thursday afternoon and Mr. Wakefield had practically kidnapped him, insisting that he come to the grocery store with him to pick out refreshments for the tree trimming Friday night.

"Tomorrow night is a special evening," Mr. Wakefield told the clerk in a hearty voice. "We're going to set up our Christmas tree, and we always like to make a little celebration out of it." He gave Steven a jovial slap on the back.

"I don't blame you," the clerk said in a cheerful tone. "It's hard to get families together these days. When you do, you have to make the most of the occasion."

Steven gritted his teeth. Tonight was a special night, too. It was the night of the big party. He had told his dad twice that he needed to be over at the Howells' by seven. But Mr. Wakefield was so wrapped up in planning their family tree trimming that he didn't seem to be in any great rush.

"Hello there, Ned," a familiar voice called out.

Steven turned and saw Mr. Howell, Joe's father, pushing a huge cart full of groceries. Mr. Howell smiled and pointed to the cart. "Just a few *last-minute things*," he said with a laugh.

Mr. Wakefield raised his eyebrows. "I never realized the Unicorns were such big eaters."

Mr. Howell chuckled. "It's not the Unicorns I'm worried about. There are at least two six-foot seniors on the basketball team, and I'm afraid if we don't provide enough food, they'll start snacking on the furniture."

Mr. Wakefield frowned. "What are the senior basketball players doing at Janet's party?"

"Didn't Steven tell you? It's Joe's party, too," Mr. Howell replied. "We told the kids we could only cope with one Christmas party, so they agreed to have their party together."

Steven was getting annoyed at the confused look on his father's face. "Dad, I *told* you I was going to a party at the Howells' tonight."

"Yes, you did," Mr. Wakefield said thoughtfully. "But when the twins said they were going to a party at the Howells', your mother and I assumed that you were just going over to help Joe with preparations. I didn't realize the twins were going to be at a party that would include high school students."

Mr. Howell frowned. "I'm sorry, Ned. I thought all the parents understood that Janet and Joe were co-hosting this party. But if it makes you feel better, my wife and I will be there from start to finish. The party will be carefully chaperoned."

Mr. Wakefield waved his hand dismissively. "Oh, I'm sure it will be. I'll just have to have a talk with Alice, and I'm sure everything will be fine."

Just then a woman pushing a full cart came hurrying around the corner and practically collided with Mr. Howell. "Oops," he cried in a cheerful tone. "I'd better get moving. It looks like I'm blocking traffic. Steven, I'll see you later. Ned, send my regards to Alice."

Mr. Wakefield smiled thinly and gave Mr. Howell a friendly but preoccupied wave.

Steven felt a little flicker of hope kindle in his chest. He knew what that look on his father's face meant. Chaperons or no chaperons, his dad wasn't too happy about the twins being at a high school party.

"The Howells are very responsible people,"

Mr. Wakefield said softly, as though he were trying to convince himself.

Steven studied his father. *Hmmm,* he thought, *he's definitely on the fence. All he needs is a little push in the right direction.* "Don't worry, Dad," he said in a reassuring voice, "I'll be there if things get too wild."

"Wild?" Mr. Wakefield repeated. "Why would things get *wild*?"

Steven lifted his shoulders in a casual shrug. "Oh, you know how it is when you get a bunch of high school guys at a party—especially a bunch of athletes."

Mr. Wakefield's frown deepened, and Steven smiled inwardly at the thought of Joe's well-behaved friends getting rowdy in someone else's house. It wouldn't happen in a million years.

But his father didn't need to know that.

"And I'm sure there won't be more than a hundred kids from the high school there anyway," Steven continued in a light tone. *More like fifty kids on the entire guest list,* he added silently, *not to mention the basketball coach and Joe's uncle.* But no need to bother his dad with those details.

"A hundred high school kids!" Mr. Wakefield exclaimed. "I don't like the sound of this."

Steven felt a twinge of guilt. *But it's not like I've told any lies,* he reasoned. All he'd said was that he knew there wouldn't be more than a hundred high school kids there. And that was the truth.

"It's one thing for the older Unicorns to be at a party with high school students. But the twins are only in sixth grade," Mr. Wakefield mused, staring into the bakery case. His face tensed. "I may be old-fashioned, but I'm not sure this is the right kind of party for the girls."

Steven fought off another surge of guilt. Sure, the twins were really looking forward to this party, but they'd get their chance to go to high school parties sooner or later. And this way, Steven wouldn't have to worry that his sisters would make a fool of him tonight.

The clerk finished tying up their pastry boxes with bright red-and-green string. "Here are your pastries, sir."

Mr. Wakefield reached into his pocket and pulled out some bills. "I know they'll be disappointed about missing the party," he said to Steven. "But maybe these cookies and pastries will cheer them up."

"Oh, I'm sure the cookies will make them feel lots better," Steven eagerly agreed. *As if a year's worth of cookies could make them feel better once you drop this bomb on them*, he added to himself.

Seven

"You look great," Jessica said on Thursday evening as she and Elizabeth stood in front of the bathroom mirror.

Elizabeth smiled at her reflection. "I feel pretty great, too." She moved over a little so that Jessica would have more mirror space. "So how did decorating go today? What's the inside scoop on the party?"

Jessica had spent two hours that afternoon helping Janet and her brother decorate the house.

"It's going to be beautiful," Jessica said excitedly. "They strung Christmas lights all over the backyard, and we decorated all the trees with balls and tinsel. So they all look like Christmas trees."

Elizabeth shivered with anticipation. It really did sound gorgeous.

"We moved all the furniture on the patio out of the way so people can dance," Jessica continued. "And Janet's mom has been baking and cooking for four days. You can't believe the amount of food they're going to have."

Jessica put on one last coat of lipstick and sighed dreamily. "In just a little while I'll be dancing with Tim Reed."

Elizabeth giggled as they walked into her bedroom to put on their shoes. "Only if you're on time for the first dance. You can't be fashionably late."

"I know," Jessica responded with a little groan. "Which means no big entrance. Think he would consider dancing the last dance with me instead of the first?"

Elizabeth shrugged. "Maybe. Just don't plan on dancing too long, because I want to talk to him about a book idea I had last night."

Mrs. Wakefield appeared in the open doorway of Elizabeth's room. She looked around, an amused expression on her face. "What's all this?"

"We're still trying to decide what to wear to the party tonight," Elizabeth answered, standing up a little straighter to model her green cashmere sweater with jeweled buttons. She knew that the color looked beautiful on her. And she had borrowed Jessica's pale-green eye shadow, which made her eyes sparkle.

Jessica looked wonderful, too. She wore a shimmering sequined top over silver silk slacks. A pair of silver platform evening shoes made her look almost as tall as Mrs. Wakefield.

Jessica pointed to three other glitzy outfits laid out on the floor. "We've narrowed it down to these five. What do you think?"

"What fun. I didn't realize that Janet's party was a costume party," Mrs. Wakefield said.

Jessica and Elizabeth exchanged looks. *What does she mean, costume party?* Elizabeth thought, feeling her stomach drop.

"It's not a costume party, Mom," Jessica responded, sounding slightly hurt.

"Oh? Then why are you dressed like this?" Mrs. Wakefield asked, coming farther into the room.

"These are our party clothes," Jessica said.

"Clothes for the party that Janet Howell is having tonight?"

The girls nodded.

"It's not a costume party?"

The girls shook their heads.

"Then I'm afraid these clothes aren't suitable, girls," Mrs. Wakefield said in a gentle but insistent tone. "Jessica, I think you should wear your green satin skirt and vest. And Elizabeth, your blue-velvet pinafore looks lovely." Mrs. Wakefield picked up a chiffon scarf and stared at it in amazement. "Where in the world did you find these, well, these *things*?"

"I bought them from a lady who makes them," Jessica said proudly. "And I don't want to wear my green satin skirt and vest."

Elizabeth took a deep breath. Disagreeing with Mrs. Wakefield about clothes was Jessica's department, but tonight Elizabeth didn't want to take her mother's advice. "And I don't want to wear my blue velvet pinafore."

Mrs. Wakefield threw Elizabeth a startled look.

"But girls," Mrs. Wakefield began exhaustedly, as if she had so many objections, she hardly knew where to begin. "Sequins! Feathers!" She picked up a brightly beaded bag. "This looks like something from a Mardi Gras parade." Her mouth formed a disapproving line. "And Elizabeth. Really! All that green eye shadow. Absolutely not. Not for a junior high party."

"But that's just it," Jessica protested. "It's not just a junior high party. There are going to be high school kids there, too."

Mrs. Wakefield frowned. "The Howells' party is for high school kids, too?"

"Didn't Steven tell you?" Elizabeth asked.

"He told me he was going to the Howells',

yes," Mrs. Wakefield said, taking a seat on Elizabeth's desk chair. "But I assumed that Joe was having a few of his friends over to pitch in and help with the refreshments and cleanup. I didn't realize the Howells—or maybe more accurately, Janet—had invited a few of the middle-school girls to a high school party."

"It's for everybody," Jessica said vehemently. "And it's not just Janet. It's her mom and dad. I mean, they know who's been invited and everything like that."

Normally, Elizabeth would have jumped in at this point and convinced their mother in her level-headed way that everything was all right. But she wasn't feeling very levelheaded at the moment. In fact, she was feeling just as panicky as Jessica was acting.

Elizabeth's head was spinning. She really hadn't tried to misrepresent the nature of the party to their mother. She just sort of assumed that she'd known what the story was. But obviously she hadn't known—and now that she did, she looked very disapproving.

Mrs. Wakefield stood abruptly. "I think I'd better call Mrs. Howell and get the straight story on this."

"Please don't," Jessica wailed.

"Please," Elizabeth echoed.

"We'll look like babies," Jessica added. "Like

we need your permission for every little thing."

"Well, I should make sure that the Howells' party *is* just a little thing," Mrs. Wakefield responded quickly. "We seem to have had a breakdown in communication that I want to clear up with Mrs.—"

They were interrupted by the sound of the front door. "Jessica! Elizabeth!" Mr. Wakefield called.

The two girls and their mother came to the top of the stairs. Mr. Wakefield stood at the bottom looking up, with Steven hovering behind him.

Mr. Wakefield looked at the twins in surprise. "You girls need to look at the calendar. It's Christmastime, not Halloween."

The twins exchanged another glance. Elizabeth didn't have the energy to respond to her father. Now *both* their parents thought they looked inappropriate for a Christmas party. Everything was going wrong.

Mr. Wakefield cleared his throat. "Alice, there's something I think we all need to discuss. I just ran into Joe and Janet's father at the grocery store. Did you realize that there are going to be high school students at Janet's party?"

"We were just getting into that," Mrs. Wakefield said, starting down the steps.

"It's not just Janet's party," Jessica clarified

again. "It's Janet and Joe's party. Which means that Janet invited her friends. And Joe invited his. *Why are you guys making such a big deal about this*?" she finished with a yell.

Mr. and Mrs. Wakefield looked up at the girls in shock and anger. Steven backed away, as if preparing to make his escape.

Not a great move, Jess, Elizabeth thought with dismay. Yelling certainly never won her and Jessica any points.

Mr. Wakefield stared up at the twins for a few moments, and Elizabeth felt her face growing white. Her dad looked really angry, and she could just feel her mother getting upset.

"Jessica," Mr. Wakefield said finally, "if you cannot talk without shouting, then you can go right to your room and stay there for the rest of the evening."

Jessica stood rigid for a moment, and Elizabeth held her breath. *Please, Jess, don't push it,* she pleaded silently.

"I'm sorry," Jessica muttered finally.

Elizabeth let her breath out in relief. Now maybe they could start to get things straightened out.

"Alice," Mr. Wakefield said, "I'm not sure that this is an appropriate party for Elizabeth and Jessica to attend. According to Mr. Howell, there will even be some seniors there."

"Seniors!" Mrs. Wakefield exclaimed. "You're right. I don't think this is something I'm comfortable with." She looked up toward the twins. "I'm sorry, girls, but it's for the best that you stay home. Since they're expecting you, I'll call Mrs. Howell and apologize for your absence. But I'm sure she'll understand when I explain that your father and I didn't realize that you would be mixing with such a mature crowd."

"MOM!" Jessica and Elizabeth cried together.

"Elizabeth Wakefield," her mother said, giving her a pained look. "I'm surprised at you. I've always felt I could safely rely on your good judgment. I can't believe you're making such a fuss."

Elizabeth felt her face burn. Did her mother think that she didn't want to have any fun? That all she wanted was to be a good little girl? She breathed deeply, trying to compose herself. "Do you think I'm such a goody-goody and stick-in-the-mud that I wouldn't want to go to a party?"

"It's not that, honey," Mrs. Wakefield said. "We just . . ."

But Elizabeth didn't wait to hear the rest. A lump rose in her throat. She ran into her room, slammed the door, and then burst into tears.

A few moments ago, she had felt incredibly grown up and beautiful. Now, when she looked in the mirror, she felt like a little kid playing dress-up.

Well, Steven doesn't have to worry now, she thought miserably. *Jessica and I won't be there to embarrass him.* All her friends would be having a blast at the party, while she, Elizabeth Wakefield, the A student, the capable, sensible editor-in-chief of the *Sixers*, would be stuck at home. And everybody would know that her mother didn't think she was mature enough to go to a party with high school kids.

Elizabeth had never felt so betrayed in her life. Her parents were always telling her how grown up she was and how proud they were of her. But actions spoke louder than words. And her parents had just sent her straight to the children's department.

Eight

Jessica sat down and stared glumly across the dinner table at Elizabeth. Both girls had cried for the past hour, and now their eyes were red and swollen.

Jessica looked miserably at her watch. Seven o'clock. Everything would be getting started right around now. Everybody at the Howells' would be starting to wonder when the twins would get there. And then, when they didn't turn up, somebody might ask Mrs. Howell where they were.

Their mother didn't think they were mature enough to come, she could hear Mrs. Howell announce.

Mandy and Mary would probably be truly sorry. But the rest of the Unicorns would just snicker and then tease Jessica about it for the rest of the year.

"Potatoes?" Mr. Wakefield asked with a smile.

"Thank you," Jessica said in a subdued tone.

After the blowup this evening, both Mr. and Mrs. Wakefield were being extra considerate and solicitous of the girls.

Jessica tightened her face as her father took her plate. She was too mad to care about how many potatoes he gave her. And she was going to stay mad for a long, long time.

"Elizabeth," Mrs. Wakefield asked, "would you like another piece of bread?"

"No, thank you," Elizabeth said quietly. Her eyes met Jessica's briefly, then dropped to her plate.

Mrs. Wakefield sighed. "Girls, I wish you two could . . ."

"Bye!" they heard Steven call from the front hall.

"Steven!" Mr. Wakefield shouted back. "Come here a moment, please."

Steven hurried through the adjoining living room and appeared in the dining room door.

"You look very nice," Mrs. Wakefield said approvingly.

"Thank you," Steven said with a shy grin.

Seeing that grin made Jessica furious. *He could at least pretend to feel bad for us, but no, we've basi-*

cally made his night, she thought. *Now he doesn't have to worry about his bratty sisters messing up his good time.*

Mr. Wakefield's face was serious. "Steven, we need to have a talk before you leave. There are going to be older kids there tonight and—"

"I can handle myself," Steven broke in.

"I know that," Mr. Wakefield answered. "But just so we're all straight on the rules, let's go over them one more time."

Steven let out a little sigh and rolled his eyes.

"No riding around in anybody's car," Mr. Wakefield began methodically. "No horseplay inside the Howells' home. You do not leave the party unless people are drinking, in which case I expect you to call me immediately and I will come pick you up *no questions asked.* Got it?"

"Got it."

"All right, then," Mrs. Wakefield said. "Have a good time and be home by eleven."

"Eleven!" Steven repeated in protest. "The invitation says *twelve* for high school kids."

"Well, your parents are inviting you to be home by eleven," Mr. Wakefield said in a pleasant but firm voice.

Jessica felt a little stab of pleasure as she looked at Steven's grumpy face. When his eyes met hers, she wrinkled her nose and stuck out her tongue.

Jessica glanced at Elizabeth, who wore a grim smile. *There*, Jessica thought with satisfaction. *Even Elizabeth thinks Steven has it coming to him.*

"Gee, Mom," Elizabeth said in a sarcastic tone, "maybe you should call Mrs. Howell and explain to her that Steven isn't mature enough to stay out until twelve."

"Shut up, Elizabeth," Steven said angrily.

Mr. Wakefield put down his water glass with an ominous thud. "If I hear one more unpleasant remark from anybody," he said, "I'm going to send that person to their room and instruct them not to come out until New Year's Day."

Jessica wished her parents would just go to their room and not come out until New Year's Day. As far as she was concerned, that would be the best Christmas present of all.

After dinner Elizabeth and Jessica sat side by side on the living room couch as Elizabeth flipped through the television schedule. "There's nothing on," she said with a sigh. "Unless you want to watch some cartoon Christmas specials."

"Little-kid stuff," Jessica said listlessly. She checked her watch. "It's seven forty-five. I'll bet they're already dancing. Tim's probably found out by now that Mom and Dad wouldn't let us go to the party."

"I know," Elizabeth responded in an even,

somber tone. "And I'm sure if he doesn't know why we're not there, Steven won't lose any time telling him."

"Hey, what's going on, Lizzie?" Jessica asked. "You're the one who's always determined to look on the bright side, remember? You're supposed to say something that will cheer me up—not agree with me."

Elizabeth let out another heavy sigh. "Ho ho ho," she said obligingly. "Is that cheerful enough for you?"

"Thanks," Jessica responded in a sarcastic tone.

"Why are you girls just sitting here doing nothing?" Mrs. Wakefield asked, appearing in the door of the den.

"We were just waiting for you to come in and tell us it's bedtime," Jessica said tightly. She looked at her watch. "Jeez, Elizabeth! It's almost eight o'clock already." She yawned elaborately. "Time to hit the hay, right?"

"Jessica!" Mrs. Wakefield said in a warning tone. "You know how I feel about sarcasm."

"Sorry," Jessica muttered, staring at her hands.

Mrs. Wakefield came over to the sofa and sat down between them, putting an arm around each twin. "I know you two are disappointed and angry," she said softly. "But this really has been difficult for your father and me, too. We never say no for the fun of it. It would have been easier to have said yes."

Jessica did her best not to roll her eyes. She didn't know how Elizabeth felt about that parental sob story, but she certainly didn't feel too sorry for her parents.

"You'll have plenty of time for high school parties when you're older," Mrs. Wakefield said. "Be patient."

Patient? Ugh! As far as Jessica was concerned, that was the dirtiest word in the English language. Patience was for people who were dull. People who were slow. People who were unimaginative.

Jessica wanted to live life in the fast lane. And the only thing stopping her was her dull, slow, and unimaginative parents.

"Enjoy being twelve as long as you *are* twelve," Mrs. Wakefield went on. "Twelve is really a very special age. You're not a child anymore. But you're not a teenager yet."

"Excuse me," Elizabeth said in a hoarse voice.

Jessica watched her sister get up and hurry out of the room, obviously on the verge of tears.

Mrs. Wakefield sighed unhappily. "Jessica, I think you'd better go see about your sister. Somehow I don't think there's anything *I* can say that will made her feel better."

You're right about that, Jessica thought, standing up and briskly leaving the room. *You've already said plenty.*

Elizabeth threw herself facedown on her bed and began to sob. She had never felt so at odds with her parents. Next to Jessica, Mrs. Wakefield had always been Elizabeth's best friend and staunch supporter. Both she and Mr. Wakefield had always placed a lot of trust in Elizabeth. When had they stopped trusting her? When had they decided that she had to be treated like a child?

She heard the door open, and pretty soon she felt someone shaking her shoulder. "Cut it out, Lizzie," Jessica ordered. "I can't believe you're getting so upset about missing a party. I mean, I'm supposed to act like that, not you."

"It's not just about missing a party," Elizabeth said, choking back her tears. She sat up and took the tissue that Jessica had ready for her. "It's about not being trusted."

"Well, for me, it's about the party. I don't know about you, but I'm not going to take this lying down."

"What do you mean?" Elizabeth demanded.

Jessica got up, went over to the bedroom door, and looked out into the hall. Then she carefully shut the door and came back over to the bed. "I say let's go to the party."

"What?" Elizabeth sat up.

"Let's tell Mom and Dad we're going to the movies or something, and then go to the Howells' instead."

"Are you totally out of your mind, Jessica?" Elizabeth protested. "The minute we get downstairs in our party clothes, Mom and Dad will know what we're doing."

"We'll take our party clothes in a backpack. We can change in the alley behind the backyard of the Howells' house. It's really dark and nobody ever goes back there except to read the water meter."

"But Steven will be there, and you know he'll tell Mom and Dad."

"If he does, we'll tell Mom and Dad about the R-rated movie he and Joe snuck into a couple of weeks ago."

Elizabeth raised her eyebrows. "Steven went to an R-rated movie?"

Jessica nodded. "I was standing on the other side of the street outside the card shop, and I saw them coming out of the theater." Her face broke into a smile. "And guess what I just happened to have with me? A camera."

"You took a picture?"

Jessica nodded. "The film is sitting in my sock drawer right now."

"But Jess, that's blackmail!" Elizabeth exclaimed in disbelief.

"Lizzie, that's insurance," Jessica countered in a bland tone.

Elizabeth smiled inwardly. She couldn't help admiring Jessica's forethought.

Then she shook her head. Whenever Jessica's wild plans began to sound logical to Elizabeth, she knew she was in trouble. "I don't know, Jess. Whatever you call it, what you did is still—"

"Hey, I know!" Jessica exclaimed, suddenly snapping her fingers. "We'll say we're going to the Christmas carnival. They'd definitely let us go to that. I mean, it's for kids."

"I don't know," Elizabeth said again. "I don't like to lie."

"Then let me do the talking," Jessica said breezily. "I don't mind lying."

"Jessica!" Elizabeth exclaimed in a shocked voice.

"It's for a good cause," Jessica reminded her. "And even if we get caught, they can't do anything to us."

"Why not?"

"Are you kidding? It's Christmas. If Mom and Dad punish us, we'll go public and make them look like really bad parents. Total ogres. All they'll do is give us some long and boring lecture about responsibility and trust and stuff like that."

Trust. Responsibility.

Those two words had always meant a lot to

Elizabeth. She had always tried to keep her word and to be trustworthy. She'd always tried to do the responsible thing.

And where had it gotten her?

Nowhere.

Here she was sitting at home, while girls who were far less responsible and trustworthy were at a party with the high school kids. With Tim Reed, the nicest high school boy that she had ever met. It wasn't fair. It wasn't fair at all.

Elizabeth's mouth formed a determined line. "OK. I'm in. Let's do it."

Nine

Elizabeth pulled on the white silk trousers and carefully placed the matching ruffled blouse in her backpack. Maybe the clothes and makeup she had on before were a little too much, but she felt confident that the outfit she'd finally chosen was wonderful. No one would think she looked silly.

She reached into her drawer and pulled out her folded-up pink warm-up suit. It was large enough on her to hide the trousers she had on underneath.

After pulling on the pants, she carefully slipped the sweatshirt on over her head so she wouldn't mess up her intricately arranged hair. It was a deceptively simple hairstyle. It looked *almost* like an ordinary ponytail, but with Jessica's help and about nine ounces of hair spray,

Elizabeth had managed to pull out and curl a dozen little tendrils around her forehead and cheeks. It looked so natural, her parents wouldn't suspect a thing.

Unfortunately, she and Jessica had had to forgo the eye shadow. Instead they both wore a little pink lip gloss—subtle enough so their parents wouldn't notice, but distinctive enough so that they looked more festive than usual.

As she examined her reflection in the mirror, Elizabeth felt a combination of excitement and the sinking feeling she got whenever she let Jessica draw her into one of her outrageous schemes.

Oh, snap out of it, she ordered herself. After all, she had already decided on a course of action. And now that it was in motion, she had to follow through with it.

"OK," Jessica whispered. "Follow me."

Jessica heaved her backpack up on her shoulder and began to lead the way downstairs.

"Hold it," Elizabeth shrieked in a whisper behind her. She felt Elizabeth's hand close over the waistband of her jeans and yank her back up on the landing.

"Your sequins are showing," Elizabeth hissed.

Jessica's hand flew around and felt the small of her back. Elizabeth was right. Her sequined blouse was bulging out between the waistband of her jeans and the ribbed bottom of her pull-over top.

With Elizabeth's help, she managed to tuck the sequined blouse more tightly into her jeans. "OK," she said. "We make one stop downstairs, say we're going to the Christmas carnival, and then split as fast as we can. Don't give them time to ask a bunch of questions. You know how easily they can make you crack."

"I will *not* crack!" Elizabeth protested.

Jessica raised her eyebrow at her sister. She knew that what they were doing definitely didn't come naturally to Elizabeth. And she couldn't let Elizabeth botch her great plan with a sudden attack of truthfulness. "I know you won't let me down, Liz."

"And I know you won't let me down," Elizabeth answered.

"Then let's move out," Jessica ordered.

The two girls descended the steps. The TV was on and Jessica could hear a variety of serious voices emanating from the living room. This was great. Her parents were watching one of those news shows where dorky-looking grown-ups got all excited and angry about some totally boring subject.

Her parents were really into those shows. And if their attention was riveted on the TV, they were a lot less likely to ask a bunch of snoopy questions.

She and Elizabeth walked into the living room. The set was on, but their parents weren't watching it.

"Mom?" she called out in a tentative voice. "Dad?"

"Were you girls looking for us?"

"*Yeowww!*" Jessica and Elizabeth screamed at the same time.

Jessica whirled around and saw her parents standing behind her and Elizabeth. They had obviously just descended the stairs themselves—which meant that they had been in their room—which was next to Jessica's—which meant they might have overheard the two girls plotting and—

"What in the world is the matter with you two?" Mr. Wakefield asked in amusement.

Only the fact that we are planning the biggest escape of our lives and we don't want you to know it, Jessica thought. She put on an innocent smile. "We thought you were in here watching TV," she explained, trying to keep her voice from quavering.

"Where are you two going?" Mrs. Wakefield nodded her head toward their backpacks.

"To the Christmas carnival," Elizabeth said immediately.

Mr. Wakefield looked at his watch.

"It's dark already," Mrs. Wakefield pointed out.

"But it's still early," Jessica said, forcing herself to sound calm and rational. "You can't make us stay home watching the news when you've already made us miss the biggest party of the whole year. Besides, the carnival is really safe. There are a lot of families there, you know. Parents. Little kids. Grandmothers . . ." She let her voice trail off, giving her parents a chance to see how reasonable this was.

Mr. and Mrs. Wakefield exchanged a glance. Then Mr. Wakefield lifted his eyebrows and gave his wife an inquisitive stare. Mrs. Wakefield appeared to be thinking something over, then she winked and smiled at Mr. Wakefield.

"We'll all go," Mr. Wakefield said heartily. "Christmastime is for families. And I say we're long overdue for an old-fashioned family outing."

Elizabeth let out a strange noise—sort of like a yip.

Mr. Wakefield frowned. "Elizabeth, did you say something?"

Jessica caught the helpless look her sister threw her. She knew Elizabeth would be counting on her to do something about this horrible turn of events. "I think we should have a family outing, too," Jessica said, thinking quickly. "But just think how hurt Steven will be if he finds out we had a family outing without him."

"Oh, Steven's a big boy," Mr. Wakefield said cheerfully. "I don't think he'll have his feelings hurt if we go to the Christmas carnival without him. What do you think, Alice?"

Mrs. Wakefield smiled. "I think Steven would consider himself far too old to go to a Christmas carnival with his parents," she finished with a laugh. "So we don't have to feel guilty about leaving him out."

Jessica glanced at Elizabeth again. It was incredible. How could their parents be so unbelievably dense? Couldn't they see she and Elizabeth weren't exactly in the mood for a family outing?

Mrs. Wakefield ran a fond hand over Elizabeth's head, smushing down the carefully teased tendrils. "Let me just run upstairs and change into something a little warmer, and we'll be on our way."

"I'll get my sweater," Mr. Wakefield said, running up the stairs behind his wife.

Elizabeth looked at Jessica, her face pale. "Now what?" she asked in a mournful tone.

Jessica threw her backpack down in disgust. "I think I'm going to be sick."

*   *   *

"Urp. Slop. Get the mop," Jessica said under her breath as she and Elizabeth lagged behind their parents at the carnival. Then she opened her mouth, stuck her tongue out, and pretended to be gagging.

"Gross, Jessica," Elizabeth snapped. "Cut it out."

"I'll cut it out when they cut it out," Jessica said gloomily.

Elizabeth had to agree that their parents' behavior was out of hand. They were acting as if they were on their first date or something. It was totally embarrassing, and Elizabeth didn't want to be seen with them.

They held hands. They shared a soda with two straws. Mr. Wakefield kissed Mrs. Wakefield's cheek. And they giggled at stuff that wasn't even funny.

Right now they were standing by something called the Tunnel of Love. The ride was a series of boats. CHRISTMAS IS FOR LOVERS, said a little sign on each boat. According to the sign over the entrance of the ride, the boats wound their way through a dark tunnel of love, which was decorated with red and green hearts.

"Alice," Mr. Wakefield said solemnly, "will you do me the honor of boating with me through the Tunnel of Love?"

Mrs. Wakefield giggled as Mr. Wakefield

slipped a coin to a balloon vendor and carefully made his choice from the bunch of helium-filled heart-shaped balloons. Mr. Wakefield took the balloon from the vendor and presented it to Mrs. Wakefield with a low and courtly bow. "For you."

Mrs. Wakefield giggled *again* and accepted the balloon with a curtsy. While she gazed happily up at it, Mr. Wakefield purchased their tickets for the ride. When Mr. Wakefield returned with the tickets and the two of them passed through the turnstile, Mrs. Wakefield smiled mistily and took Mr. Wakefield's hand.

Mr. Wakefield smiled, too. "We'll be back soon," he called out gaily over his shoulder. "You can meet us at the refreshment stand."

Jessica and Elizabeth stared glumly after them. "Are you thinking what I'm thinking?" Elizabeth asked.

"Yeah, I'm thinking this doesn't exactly feel like a family outing," Jessica answered.

"In fact, they're pretty much treating us like tagalongs," Elizabeth added. "We might as well be out with Steven and one of his girlfriends. It's like they're totally ignoring us."

"Well, I don't know about you," Jessica said, "but I sure wouldn't want anybody to see me here with my parents."

"Yeah, they're pretty embarrassing," Elizabeth

conceded. "But it's the principle of the thing. I mean, since they insisted on coming along, they could at least make an effort to include us so that *we'd* get the chance to ignore *them*. Now I'll bet people think the only reason they brought us along was because they couldn't get a baby-sitter."

"Well, look at it this way," Jessica said. "At least we're free to go off on our own for a little."

Elizabeth fell into step beside Jessica and looked around as they made their way through the crowd. The carnival didn't look magical, the way it had before. It looked cheap and tacky. The snow on the roofs of the game booths looked exactly like what it was—drifts of molded plastic that had been spray-painted white and sprinkled with glitter.

The Christmas trees that marked the entrance to every ride didn't smell fresh, green, and piney. They smelled musty, sort of like old, wet newspapers. It was an appropriate smell for fake trees that probably spent most of the year in storage.

The whole place looked so depressing that Elizabeth wished they hadn't come. She would have preferred to stay home and read.

"Let's get some chestnuts," Jessica suggested.

Elizabeth nodded. Some chestnuts might be a good snack.

"The last time we were here, the chestnut cart

was over this way." Jessica turned a corner, and Elizabeth followed along.

They passed a lot of familiar landmarks. The ticket window for the merry-go-round. The ornament booth. The "California Christmas" Santa—a big plastic Santa in a red velvet suit riding a surfboard with a sack of toys slung over his shoulder. The toys were for sale, but they looked as though they had been sitting around for years. The paper part of the packaging was dog-eared, and the plastic part was cloudy.

Jessica looked around for the chestnut cart. "I thought it was right around here. But I guess I was wrong."

"No, you're not," Elizabeth said suddenly. "Look. There's the wishing well. Remember how the chestnut man threw the coin into the well and wished us an unforgettable Christmas?"

"Yeah, right. A lot of good that did," Jessica said bitterly. "Somehow I don't think this story is going to have a happy ending."

"He said unforgettable and happy weren't always the same thing," Elizabeth reminded her sister.

"Then forget the chestnuts," Jessica announced. "I'll spend the money on my own Christmas wish." She dug into her pocket for a coin.

"Me, too," Elizabeth said, pulling a quarter from the pocket of her warm-up suit. "I wish that—"

"*Stop!*" Jessica yelled.

Elizabeth jumped. "What's the matter?"

"Nothing's the matter," Jessica explained in a more normal voice. "I just wanted to remind you not to tell me your wish or it won't come true."

"That's the way birthday wishes work," Elizabeth said.

"That's the way *all* wishes work," Jessica retorted.

Elizabeth rolled her eyes. Sometimes Jessica was so ridiculously superstitious. Then she smiled. *Look who's talking. I'm standing next to a completely phony wishing well about to throw away good money for a wish. So I guess I might as well push the superstition to the limit.*

Elizabeth closed her eyes and tensed all of her muscles. *I wish I were grown up.*

Jessica closed her eyes and took a deep breath, preparing to release her coin and make her wish.

Plink! she heard, signifying that Elizabeth had just dropped her coin in the well.

A chilly breeze lifted Jessica's hair away from her face. She shivered and took another deep breath. *I wish I were grown up.*

Plink! went the coin as it hit the surface of the water.

A second, even colder breeze blew past. Jessica opened her eyes and saw that Elizabeth stood shivering with her eyes shut tightly. The breeze was tossing and pulling at the little tendrils that the two of them had so carefully curled around Elizabeth's face.

Jessica tucked her hands inside her sleeves and looked around. Nobody else seemed to be cold. Hadn't anyone else felt that breeze?

She turned her attention back to Elizabeth. She was probably wishing for world peace or something like that. "Enough, Elizabeth," Jessica said. "I don't think you're going to get a million dollars' worth of wishes for a quarter."

Elizabeth laughed as she opened her eyes and looked across the well at Jessica. Then, as suddenly as it had arrived, the breeze disappeared.

"Hey, Wakefield! . . . oooo . . . at . . . mph . . . ti . . ."

Steven turned to see who was shouting into his ear. It was Tim Reed. But the music was blaring so loudly that it made conversation difficult.

Not that Steven was complaining. He loved rock and roll cranked up to an earsplitting level. In fact, he loved everything about the party.

So why did he have a big lump in his stomach?

The band was great, and the food was unbelievable. Silver trays holding mini-hamburgers, mini–hot dogs, mini-enchiladas, and mini–egg rolls covered the dining room table. Tall crystal jars contained at least five different kinds of cookies and Christmas chocolates.

The band was playing in the living room, and the double doors to the patio were open so that the kids could use the patio as a dance floor.

Steven took a Christmas cookie and bit into it.

It was strange, but the cookie didn't seem to have much taste. It felt crumbly and dry. In fact, none of the food had seemed to have much taste.

Tim leaned forward and yelled right into his ear. "Where are Jessica and Elizabeth? I haven't seen them all evening."

Suddenly, the music seemed off-key somehow. Steven didn't feel up to explaining, so he just shrugged his shoulders.

"Great food!" Tim yelled into Steven's ear as he made a quick pass around the dining room table, loading up his plate before he came back over to stand beside Steven.

He chewed enthusiastically and nodded his head to the music. *"Why aren't you dancing?"* he yelled after swallowing a bite of hamburger.

Steven shrugged again. He wasn't sure. There

were lots of pretty girls there, and he knew most of them. But somehow he just didn't feel like dancing.

He reached into the jar and picked up another Christmas cookie. This one was in the shape of a Unicorn—in honor of Janet's guests.

Thinking about Janet made him think about Jessica. And thinking about Jessica made him think about Elizabeth. And the thought of Jessica and Elizabeth made the lump in his stomach feel even heavier.

Tons of people had asked about them—and not just the middle-schoolers, either. A lot of the high school kids seemed to be really sorry they weren't there.

Suddenly, Steven realized that he was sorry that they weren't there, too. The party was great. Steven didn't feel ill at ease at all. Everybody was friendly, and the middle-schoolers and the high school kids were hitting it off fine.

Having the twins there would have been a blast. After all, they were pretty and friendly and funny and . . . and . . . and . . . he suddenly realized he was proud of them.

A lump rose in his throat. *I'm the reason the twins aren't here having a great time*, he thought unhappily. *I totally spoiled it for them, and for no good reason.* He felt so bad about the way he'd acted that he almost felt like crying.

"Having a good time?" Joe yelled as he came into the dining room with another tray of cookies.

No, thought Steven. *I'm not having a good time at all. In fact, I'm having such a bad time, I think I'll go home.*

Steven quickly thanked Joe and made his way to the door. It wasn't that late. Maybe he and the twins could sit up and watch some old movie together.

He'd tell them that the party had been really boring and no fun at all. That way, they wouldn't have to feel bad about missing it.

I'll make it up to them somehow, he vowed. As he began walking home, he had an idea. Next week he would take his sisters out for a pizza. And he would invite Tim Reed to come along.

Ten

"This has been the most miserable evening of my whole life," Jessica muttered as she and Elizabeth climbed into the back of the Jeep after the carnival.

"Mine, too," Elizabeth agreed softly.

"And they haven't even noticed we're not having a good time," Jessica added.

"Yes, we have," Mrs. Wakefield said as she got into her side of the Jeep and buckled her seat belt.

"We have what?" Mr. Wakefield asked as he slid into the front seat behind the wheel.

"Noticed that the girls weren't having a good time," Mrs. Wakefield told him.

Mr. Wakefield glanced at the girls in the rear-view mirror. "I wish you two would stop pouting over the party."

"We're not pouting," Elizabeth protested.

"You certainly look like you're pouting," Mrs. Wakefield said, with a note of amusement in her voice.

"We're *not* pouting," Jessica repeated.

Mr. Wakefield glanced in the rearview mirror again. "Oh, excuse me," he said with a look of mock chagrin. "How silly of me. Of course you're not pouting. You're *scowling*." He looked at Mrs. Wakefield and shrugged his shoulders. "I make that mistake all the time."

Mrs. Wakefield began to laugh in a high-pitched, girlish way.

Elizabeth and Jessica looked at each other, both frowning deeply.

"OK, OK," their father said. "We're sorry we invited ourselves along to the carnival, but what do we have to do to make it up to you?"

Quit humoring us as if we were ten years old, Elizabeth thought.

Jessica crossed her arms and bit her lip.

"Think they'll get over this by tomorrow evening?" Mr. Wakefield asked his wife. "If they won't talk, who are you going to argue with over the Christmas tree?"

Again, Mrs. Wakefield let out a delighted laugh.

Usually Elizabeth loved the sound of her mother's laughter, but tonight it sounded awful.

Because tonight, for the first time in her life, Elizabeth felt that her mother was laughing at her, not with her.

"Talk about strange," Jessica said, walking into the bathroom that she and Elizabeth shared.

"What's strange?" Elizabeth reached for a towel and began to dry her face and hands.

"Mom just checked Steven's room, and he's already home and asleep." Jessica reached for the soap and bent her face over the sink. "Think he got sick or something?"

Elizabeth scowled. "I hope so."

Elizabeth awoke with a start and sighed with relief when she saw the first rays of early-morning sunlight pouring in through the window. She blinked her eyes against the glare, feeling grateful to be awake.

She had been dreaming. Actually, she had been having a nightmare. In her nightmare she had spent the whole night trying to escape the Christmas carnival and get to the party. She *had* to get to the party. She had to deliver an important message. But every time she tried to leave the carnival, something stood in her way. Her parents. Steven. The man that sold the hot chestnuts.

Elizabeth pushed back the blanket and pulled at the neck of her gown. She was hot—too hot.

And the neck of her gown was so tight it made her feel as if she were choking.

Her fingers fumbled with the top button as she tried to unbutton it. After a moment or two of tugging, the button popped off as if it had been under a great deal of strain.

The relief she felt was almost immediate, but as she sat up to look for the lost button, she noticed that the cuffs of her long-sleeved cotton gown were practically up to her elbows.

I must be half-asleep or something, she thought as she yawned and stretched her arms out wide.

Riiip!

The shoulder seams on either side of her gown tore and left a large gaping hole across the back.

What in the . . . She jumped out of bed and her mouth fell open. Her gown usually hung below her ankles. Now it barely reached her knees.

Something else was different. Something she couldn't quite put her finger on. Something that just didn't look right. What was it?

She put a toe inside one of her slippers, and that's when she realized what was different. It was her feet. They were enormous!

Oh no! she thought. It must be one of those weird growth-spurt things. In certain strange cases people's feet grew to full size before the rest of their body had a chance to catch up.

I look like I'm wearing skis, Elizabeth thought as

she ran toward the bathroom that connected her room to Jessica's. This was a case for Jessica Wakefield, Sweet Valley's leading expert on tabloid stories.

Jessica was always telling people of some story she had read about a baby who was believed to be Martian because he had been born with two antennae. Stories about men who weighed nine hundred pounds and had to be rescued from their homes with a forklift. Stories about women whose fingernails grew a foot long.

Elizabeth hoped that Jessica might have heard of something like this before. And maybe she would know what to do about it.

"Jessica!" Elizabeth called out as she entered the bathroom. "Wake up and . . . *Arrgghhh!*"

Elizabeth practically leaped into the air, she was so surprised and frightened. There was a strange lady in the bathroom. Elizabeth saw her in the mirror, standing behind her.

"Who are you, and what are you doing in my bathroom?" Elizabeth demanded, whirling to face her.

But the strange young woman vanished. Elizabeth reached for the shower curtain with a shaking hand. The woman must have jumped into the tub and hidden in its folds.

"Come out!" she ordered, pulling the curtain away.

But there was nobody in the bathroom.

Elizabeth began to feel a bit dizzy, as if she might be about to faint. Something strange was going on. She was having hallucinations. What could she possibly have eaten that would make her hallucinate? *Maybe I'll just splash some water on my face, and everything will be all—*

As she turned toward the sink, she let out an earsplitting scream. The young woman was back, peering into the mirror with a drawn and frightened face.

But Elizabeth's reflection was nowhere to be seen.

She heard Jessica's feet hit the floor. "Elizabeth?" she called out in a deep and husky voice, as if she were coming down with something.

Elizabeth turned and leaned against the counter. Come to think of it, her own voice had sounded strange, too. Maybe it was the acoustics in the bathroom.

Jessica opened the door.

"Arrgghhh!" Elizabeth screamed.

It wasn't Jessica on the other side of the bathroom door. It was the strange young woman. And she looked as horrified to see Elizabeth as Elizabeth was to see her.

*   *   *

"*Arrgghhhh!*" Jessica screamed, terrified at the sight of the blond lady standing in her bathroom. "Who are you?"

But the strange blond lady was too busy screaming herself to answer. "*Who are you?*" she shouted.

"Who am *I?*" Jessica cried in a shaking voice. "Who are *you?*"

But instead of answering the question, the blond lady shut the bathroom door and locked it with a click.

Jessica backed away, breathing hard, her heart thundering. That woman had been in Elizabeth's room. And it looked as though she was wearing one of Elizabeth's nightgowns—what was left of it, anyway.

Jessica shivered involuntarily. Where was Elizabeth? Had that woman done something with her?

Quick as lightning, Jessica ran out into the hall. She would burst through the bedroom doorway, take the woman by surprise, and rescue Elizabeth.

Jessica threw open Elizabeth's bedroom door and ran in. But Elizabeth was nowhere to be seen. And when the blond lady saw her, she opened her mouth and screamed again.

Her legs shaking, Jessica dashed into the hallway and back into her own room.

Where was Elizabeth? she thought again, her panic rising. What had that blond lady done with her sister?

What has that woman done with Jessica? Elizabeth thought, sitting on her bed and trembling.

Panic rose in her throat, and it was all she could do not to start screaming. But screaming was probably the wrong thing to do. Especially if that lady was an escaped lunatic.

She wanted to go get help, but she knew she couldn't leave Jessica alone in there. Not with a strange woman who, for some weird reason, seemed to be wearing Jessica's pajamas, the blue ones that Elizabeth had given her for her last birthday.

Elizabeth ran into the bathroom. She unlocked the door that led to Jessica's room and burst in—coming face-to-face with the intruder.

"Arrgghhh!" the woman screamed.

But this time, Elizabeth wasn't going to run away. She was going to face the lady down. Slowly, she began to step toward the strange young woman.

The strange young woman seemed to have decided the same thing. She was approaching Elizabeth in the same, slow, cautious manner in which Elizabeth was approaching her.

Their eyes met, and Elizabeth felt another strange sensation. It was the shock of recognition.

She was looking at herself!

Elizabeth saw a flash of images in quick succession. She saw the Christmas carnival. The elf with the chestnut cart. A burst of magical light. A wishing well. Herself making a wish. *I wish I were grown up.* The concentric circles on the water where the coin had penetrated the surface. A sudden, chilly wind.

"Jessica?" she asked in a whisper.

"Elizabeth?" the lady gasped.

As one, Elizabeth and Jessica turned their heads toward the mirror that hung over Jessica's dressing table.

"Arrgghhh!" they screamed together.

Eleven

"Jessica! Elizabeth! What's going on in there?"

Jessica grabbed Elizabeth's arm and yanked her in the direction of the bathroom. "Nothing, Mom," she called out. "It's just me and Elizabeth horsing around."

She pushed Elizabeth into the bathroom. "But . . . but . . ." Elizabeth sputtered.

"Not now," Jessica whispered. "We'll talk later. After we get rid of Mom."

"Jessica?" Mrs. Wakefield called out. "Your voice sounds hoarse. Are you getting a cold?"

"No," Jessica replied in a voice much deeper and throatier than her own. She cleared her throat. "No," she said again, forcing her voice into a higher register.

"Maybe I'd better have a look at you,"

Mrs. Wakefield said in a worried tone.

With horror, Jessica saw the knob of her door turning. Just as the door began to swing open, she jumped into the bathroom and shut the door. She gestured frantically to Elizabeth to turn on the tap in the bathtub.

A roaring noise filled the bathroom.

"Jessica!" her mother called out from the other side of the bathroom door. "Come out and let me feel your head. If you've got a fever I want you to go back to bed."

"I'm in the tub," Jessica said, exchanging a horrified look with Elizabeth. She cleared her throat again. "I feel fine," she added in a high childish voice. "My voice sounds funny because I just woke up."

"All right, then, I'm going downstairs to start breakfast. Come down when you get out of the tub. And bring Elizabeth."

Mrs. Wakefield left the room, closing Jessica's bedroom door behind her.

Immediately, the girls turned to the mirror again and stared at themselves in amazement.

"It can't be true," Elizabeth whispered.

"But it is," Jessica said in an awed voice. She lifted her hand and ran it over her face. "Unbelievable," she whispered. "But true."

"What happened?" Elizabeth demanded. "How did we both get this way?"

A slow smile spread over Jessica's face. "I think I got my wish."

Elizabeth stared at her. "You wished you were grown up?"

Jessica nodded, staring back. "Did you?"

"Yeah," Elizabeth said mournfully. "*Now* what are we going to do?"

Jessica straightened her posture and squared her shoulders.

Riiip!

The entire sleeve of Jessica's pajama top tore off. Jessica examined herself, then Elizabeth. Both of them were dressed in rags. "The first thing we do is get dressed," she announced. "And we'd better move fast before Mom decides she needs to come up here and take my temperature. Put on anything that's too big for you—that used to be too big for you, that is."

Jessica ran into her room and made a frantic lunge for her bottom drawer, where she kept clothes that were a little too big. She reached for the warm-up suit that Aunt Helen had sent a few months ago.

She peeled the torn pajamas off and stepped into the pants. "*Ugh!*" she said out loud. The pants were way too tight. She felt as if she were being strangled from the waist down.

She tried to pull the top down over her head, but it got stuck. It was like a straitjacket. And the harder she struggled, the tighter the straitjacket became.

In panic, she strained with every muscle to get the top on.

Riiiip!

The seams gave way, and Jessica collapsed on her bed, defeated. After a moment, she got up and stuffed the remains of the warm-up suit back into the drawer.

Then she ran to the closet and took a quick inventory. But it looked as if nothing in her closet was going to fit. *There's only one solution*, she thought. *I'll have to raid Mom's closet.* She should probably pick up something for Elizabeth, too.

Jessica wrapped a towel around her upper body and ran out of her room. She hurried down the hall toward her parents' bedroom and screeched to a stop when she realized the upstairs hall closet was open and someone was in there.

It was her dad. She could hear him whistling and muttering to himself. "Now, where's my green sweater?" he murmured absentmindedly. "Maybe it's in my bureau."

Jessica crossed her fingers. *Ideally, he's so distracted and absentminded that he's not too tuned in to details right now.*

Jessica just barely had time to hide behind the open closet door before her father turned and

walked out of the closet and into the master bedroom.

Slowly and stealthily, Jessica crept around the
door and stepped into the closet. She pulled the
door almost shut and tugged the overhead cord
that turned out the closet light.

Through the crack in the door, she watched as
her father reappeared wearing his green cardi-
gan. As soon as he had descended to the landing
of the steps, Jessica whipped out of the closet and
ducked into her parents' room.

She went straight to the closet. And even
though her heart was pounding in her chest, and
she had no idea whatsoever what had happened,
she felt a strange surge of excitement. She had
been looking forward to the day she could raid
her mother's closet for years.

Jessica pulled out Mrs. Wakefield's beautiful
black jumpsuit and quickly changed into it. She
reached for the belt. It was a little big but nothing
too noticeable. Then she slipped her feet into her
mother's nicest black pumps.

They were a perfect fit—well, almost perfect.
They were a little tight, but so what? They looked
great with the outfit.

Jessica wished there were a full-length mirror
handy, but there wasn't. She would have to wait
until she got back into her own room to admire
herself.

First things first, though.

She sorted swiftly through her mother's suits, dresses, and slacks. *Hmmm, what would Elizabeth like?* she wondered. *I'd better take a large selection just in case.*

Moments later, Jessica backed out of Mrs. Wakefield's closet with her arms full of clothes and shoes and . . . "Oomph!" Jessica let out a little grunt as she backed into something firm. That something backed away in alarm.

"What are you doing in my house?"

Jessica whirled around and saw Mrs. Wakefield staring at her, her face a mixture of horror and fear.

"Mom, let me explain," Jessica began.

"Mom?" Mrs. Wakefield cried out. "Who are you? What are you doing here?"

Before Jessica could say another word, her mother had run out the door. "Ned! Ned!" she cried, running down the steps.

Jessica bounded after her and practically fell over a very sleepy and very astonished Steven, who was just emerging from his room. "Perfect timing, Steven," she said sarcastically.

Steven squinted uncertainly and rubbed his eyes. "Who are *you?*" he asked.

"Long story," Jessica snapped, hurrying into her room and shutting the door. "Elizabeth!" she shouted. "Get in here!"

*   *   *

Elizabeth tensed at the sound of Jessica's screaming. She had locked herself in the bathroom to hide out from her mother. Fortunately, Mrs. Wakefield hadn't come into her bedroom, but obviously something else had gone wrong. Elizabeth unlocked the door and opened it a crack. "What happened?" she demanded.

"Mom saw me," Jessica said. She threw the armful of clothes in Elizabeth's direction and ran for the door. "Find something that fits, and then climb out the window and meet me around the corner."

"Where are you going?" Elizabeth asked.

"I'm going to distract them so they don't see you."

Elizabeth nodded and immediately reached for her mother's blue tweed suit and blouse. It took her no more than ten seconds to get her clothes on, find a pair of flats, and get everything zipped and buttoned. The hem was a little shorter than she had expected. *My gosh*, she thought in surprise. *We're taller than Mom.*

She ran into her bedroom, threw up her window, and stepped out on the ledge. Very carefully, she made her way over the roof until she was standing over the front door of the house.

When she looked down, she saw Jessica run out the door and cut across the yard.

The next thing she saw was the top of her father's head. "Wait!" he shouted after her. "Who are you? What were you doing in here?" As Jessica ran out of sight, he dashed back into the house.

Elizabeth made her way to the side of the house and then climbed carefully down the stone section of the outside wall.

Once her feet were on the ground, she started running.

And she didn't look back.

Twelve

Jessica paced back and forth on the sidewalk. She and Elizabeth had run nearly a mile and had paused to catch their breath and consider their next move. "This is incredible," Jessica said. "This is amazing. We should call the talk shows right now. They'll all want to book us."

"Jessica . . ." Elizabeth began.

But Jessica continued to pace, too wound up to be interrupted. "And the newspapers. Just think of all the stuff they'll write about us." She stopped in mid-pace and held up her hands, as if she were laying out a headline. "TWELVE-YEAR-OLD TWINS AGE TEN YEARS OVERNIGHT."

"Ten years? Do you think we're twenty-two?"

Jessica stopped and looked carefully at her

sister. "Probably not. More like nineteen or twenty. But Liz, we look *great!*"

"Really?"

"Would I lie?"

"Sure."

"To my own twin?"

"Jessica!" Elizabeth said in an ominous tone.

Jessica knew that tone. It was the tone Elizabeth used when she was about to pull out her laundry list of Jessica's blunders, bloopers, and bleepers.

"OK, OK!" Jessica said hastily. "I guess I've probably stretched the truth once or twice. But not this time. I'm telling you, Elizabeth, you're beautiful. And if I'm even half as pretty as you are, I'm thrilled."

"You do look beautiful," Elizabeth said musingly, staring at her sister. "I still can't get over it."

Jessica threw her shoulders back and thrust her chest forward. "Look at this," she cried. "I've got a bust."

Elizabeth blushed. "I know. I couldn't help noticing that our figures are . . . well . . . pretty full."

"Not fat, though?" Jessica asked in a worried voice.

Elizabeth shook her head. "Not fat. Just shapely."

"I don't know about you," Jessica said, patting her firm stomach happily. "But I feel relieved. We . . . I mean *I* . . . do eat an awful lot of junk food. Sometimes at night I lie awake and worry that I'll grow up to be fat. But I didn't. I mean, I won't. I mean I'm not." She shook her head in bewilderment. "Boy, this is confusing."

A bright-red sports car came around the corner and immediately slowed.

"Who's that?" Elizabeth asked nervously. "And why is he looking at us like that?"

Jessica elbowed Elizabeth gleefully. "That's Barney, Alex Betner's older brother. He's in college. And he's looking at us like that because we're gorgeous." She smiled at Barney and fluttered her fingers in a flirtatious wave.

The driver kept his head swiveled toward the girls and smiled broadly as he returned the wave.

Honk! Honk!

"Hey, look out!" Elizabeth screamed.

Barney was so busy looking at the girls that he had let his car drift into the wrong lane and was now on a collision course with an oncoming van.

Screech!

The van careened into the other lane and missed the red sports car by inches.

"Idiot!" the van driver yelled.

Barney jerked the wheel of his car, pulling back into the right lane. Then, as if to show the girls that he was still hot stuff, he revved his engine and took the next corner on two wheels.

"He *is* an idiot," Elizabeth said.

"But he's a cute idiot," Jessica pointed out.

Elizabeth rolled her eyes. "He's in college, Jess."

"Which means he's too old for me."

Elizabeth grinned. "Too old *and* too young." She began to laugh.

"You're right," Jessica said with a gasp. Then she sat down and began to laugh, too. "This is the greatest thing that's ever happened to us. Just think about it, Lizzie. We're grown-ups. We can do anything we want to. *Anything.* Eat what we want to. Go to bed when we want to. Go to any party that we want to."

Elizabeth frowned. "I think you're forgetting something, Jess."

"What?" Jessica demanded.

Elizabeth stood up and turned out the pockets of her mother's suit jacket. "Well, we have no money, for one thing." She began to count on her fingers. "And no family. And no friends. No place to go. No place to stay. No place to sleep." Her voice broke, and a small tear began to roll down her cheek.

"Come on, Lizzie," Jessica begged, digging around in her pockets for a tissue. "Don't get upset. We don't know how long this is going to last. We may hear a loud pop sound any minute, and the next thing we know, we'll be twelve again. So while we've . . . aha!" Jessica located a little flat pack of tissues. She whisked one out and offered it to Elizabeth. "So while we've got these great grown-up bodies, let's try to have some fun."

"I guess I'm too hungry to have fun," Elizabeth said with a sniff.

As soon as Elizabeth said the word *hungry*, Jessica's own stomach began to rumble. As excited as she was, she had to admit she was hungry, too. And there was a delicate smell in the air, a smell Jessica recognized—doughnuts!

"Come on," Jessica said. "We're two blocks away from the Sweet Valley Bakery."

"But we don't have any money."

"We'll see if we can work in exchange for some doughnuts," Jessica said. "Come on."

Jessica linked her arm through Elizabeth's, and the two girls quickly walked the four blocks to the Sweet Valley Bakery, arriving just as a bakery truck came whizzing out of the parking lot. As it passed, the smell of the fresh doughnuts, loaded in the back for delivery to all the local groceries and diners, drifted in the air.

A chain-link fence surrounded the parking lot, and the girls walked up and peered through the links. Several Sweet Valley Bakery delivery trucks were sitting in the parking lot ready to roll. A male supervisor with a clipboard stood in the parking lot making notes.

"What do you think?" Jessica whispered.

"I don't know," Elizabeth whispered back. "What kind of work could we do in exchange for doughnuts? Maybe we would have better luck if we went to a restaurant and offered to wash dishes."

"Wash dishes!" Jessica exclaimed. "Any twelve-year-old can wash dishes. We're grown-ups, and I think we should work in positions of authority. I want a job where I can boss people around."

"Jessica!"

"I'm serious. I've been a little kid my whole life—which means I've spent my whole life letting other people boss me around. It's about time I'm the boss*er* instead of the boss*ee*."

"Grier!" shouted the man with the clipboard.

There was an answering honk from one of the trucks. The man with the clipboard waved his hand, and the truck pulled out of its parking place and moved toward the exit.

"Hansen! Michaels! Goldman!"

There were three beeps in response. And then, one by one, each van pulled out of the parking lot and into the street.

"Morgan!" the supervisor with the clipboard shouted.

There was no answering beep.

"Morgan," the supervisor shouted again. He looked up and frowned in confusion.

"Morgan's not here today," one of the men shouted from the cab of his truck.

The supervisor made an impatient motion with his head. "How am I supposed to fill all our orders with one of my truck drivers gone?"

There was no answer from the remaining truck drivers.

He frowned at his clipboard. "Well, everybody get going. The breakfast crowd is going to be hitting the diners in about half an hour, and we're already half an hour behind schedule."

Two more trucks pulled out of the parking lot, leaving one truck behind.

"Did you hear that?" Jessica said eagerly. "They need a truck driver."

Elizabeth looked at her sister with dismay. "Oh, no," she said.

"How hard can it be to drive a truck?"

"Don't even think about it," Elizabeth warned.

"Yoo-hoo!" Jessica called out.

"Jessica, no!"

"Yoo-hoo! Excuse me!" Jessica trilled.

When the supervisor looked up, Jessica straightened her shoulders and gave him a dazzling smile.

The guy's face turned beet red, and he dropped his clipboard. When it hit the pavement, his papers flew out in every direction. "Yes, ma'am?" he stuttered, struggling to retrieve his clipboard and chase the papers that were blowing across the parking lot.

Jessica elbowed Elizabeth and giggled. Elizabeth shot Jessica a warning look and then bent to pick up a couple of sheets of paper. "Jessica, don't," she whispered fiercely.

Jessica approached the supervisor. "I couldn't help overhearing," she said as he stood up. "It just so happens that my sister and I are looking for a job so we can make a little extra Christmas money. We would be happy to deliver some of your doughnuts."

The guy swallowed nervously. "Really?"

"Yes, really," Jessica replied brightly.

He appeared to think about it for a moment. "Well, that would be great. It's our busiest season. We can't afford to lose any of our customers. So I take it you drive a tr—"

"The only problem is," Jessica broke in with a smile, "we couldn't possibly deliver a product that we didn't know anything about. And frankly, I've heard one or two disturbing things about your doughnuts."

The supervisor's face darkened. "Like what?" he demanded.

"Well," Jessica said, cocking her head to the side and placing a thoughtful finger to her temple, "a friend of mine said she thought your doughnuts were a little dry and stale-tasting."

"Dry and stale-tasting!" he exclaimed. "That's ridiculous. The Sweet Valley Bakery bakes its own doughnuts every day before dawn and delivers them to the grocery stores and restaurants by the time they open. There are no fresher doughnuts in the whole state of California. And if you don't believe me, you can taste one yourself."

"That's a good idea. I'd love to taste one," Jessica said sweetly.

The supervisor opened up the back of the remaining truck, and the smell was so delicious and intoxicating, Jessica almost fainted. He pulled out a box of doughnuts, opened it, and offered it to them.

The girls each took two and crammed them into their mouths.

"Ommmph . . . fhommmpphh . . . mmmhhh," Jessica said.

"I beg your pardon?"

Jessica swallowed hard and smacked her lips. "Delicious," she pronounced. "But you can't judge a whole batch by one or two. If you don't mind, I'd like to conduct a random sampling."

The supervisor's eyes widened a bit as Jessica reached into the back of the truck, opened another box, and removed two more doughnuts. She stuffed one in her mouth and handed the other to Elizabeth.

"Mmmmm," Jessica said as she chewed on a mouthful of sweet, fluffy doughnut. "Just as I thought. This one is not as good."

"Not as good!" The supervisor grabbed another box, opened it up, and offered it to them. "Maybe the first two dulled your palate. Try the chocolate ones."

"If you insist." Jessica snatched another two doughnuts, crammed one in her mouth, and offered the other to Elizabeth.

Elizabeth's mouth was still full from the last doughnut. Her cheeks were puffed out, and her eyes were large and a little glassy. She shook her head at the doughnut, so Jessica stuffed it into her own mouth.

"Yes," she said thickly. "You were absolutely right. These doughnuts are delicious, and it would be an honor to deliver them."

"Great, then. We'll do the paperwork right now and have you on your way in half an hour. All I need to see is your Social Security card, driver's license, previous employer, a bank reference, and proof of citizenship. None of that's a problem, right?"

"Right," Jessica confirmed while throwing a desperate and questioning look toward Elizabeth.

But all she got from Elizabeth was a blank stare and a sudden, loud belch.

Thirteen

"Think hard, Mrs. Wakefield. Are you sure you have never seen the woman before?" the police detective asked on Friday morning in the Wakefields' living room.

"Yes," Mrs. Wakefield said in a shaking voice. "I'm sure."

The detective turned toward Steven. "But you say she called you by name?"

Steven nodded. "Yeah. She called me Steven."

"And you have never seen the woman before, either?"

"No. I've never see her before. But there was something . . ." Steven broke off and bit his lip. There had been something oddly familiar about the woman. Something about the inflection of her voice and the way she moved her head.

"Steven?" Mr. Wakefield prompted. "Did you have something else to say?"

"I couldn't help thinking she reminded me of somebody. But I don't know who."

"Was anything stolen?" the detective continued.

"Just a few clothes and shoes," Mrs. Wakefield said.

"No purses, wallets, or jewelry?"

"No, there wasn't," Mr. Wakefield answered, an impatient edge to his voice. "And even if there were, it's our girls that we're concerned about."

The police detective continued scribbling on his pad and nodded his head.

"Excuse me, sir." A uniformed policeman entered the living room from the kitchen. "I've checked all the doors and windows. There's no sign of tampering."

The detective lifted one eyebrow and looked around at the Wakefields. "Are you *sure* that none of you let this woman in?"

Steven shook his head, and so did Mr. and Mrs. Wakefield.

The detective gave them a wry look and flipped his pad shut. "Then I'm going to guess this was some kind of prank and maybe your girls were in on it. Some of the sororities from the SVU campus initiate their pledges just before the holidays. So we see a lot of silly hazing stunts this time of year."

"Detective!" Mr. Wakefield argued. "Our girls are in the sixth grade. They don't *know* any college girls. I think you're being a little hasty in dismissing this incident as a hazing prank."

"I'll tell you what," the detective said, standing up. "If you find that anything important is missing—money or jewelry or things of that nature—give me a call."

The detective pulled a card from his front pocket and handed it to Mrs. Wakefield. "Come on, Officer Manning, let's get down to the station and do the paperwork, though frankly I don't think this is anything to get too worried about."

The detective and Officer Manning started toward the front door.

Steven stared after the men in disbelief. A total stranger had been running around their house this morning stealing his mother's clothes, his sisters were gone, and the police were just treating it like a big yawn.

"Wait!" Mr. Wakefield ordered.

"What about my girls?" Mrs. Wakefield shouted.

The detective shrugged slightly. "They were here last night?"

"Right," Mr. Wakefield said. "Mrs. Wakefield and I took the girls to the Christmas carnival.

Then the four of us came home and went right to bed."

The detective shot a look at Steven. "Did you go with them to the carnival?"

Steven felt a pang of guilt. "No, sir. I was at a party."

"OK, let me see if I've got this straight. The last time you saw the girls was last night. And this morning, they were gone. Had their beds been slept in?"

"Yes," Mrs. Wakefield said, wringing her hands.

Mr. Wakefield stepped closer and put his arm around her. "It'll be OK," he said softly. "They'll find the girls."

"Well, if their beds were slept in, isn't it possible that they simply got up early and went out?"

"Elizabeth, yes," Steven said. "Jessica, no. She's not exactly what you'd call an early bird."

"Neither of them would have left without saying anything. That woman has done something with my children," Mrs. Wakefield insisted.

The detective looked at his watch. "It's only eight thirty. Could they have run away?"

"No!" Mr. and Mrs. Wakefield exclaimed at the same time.

Mrs. Wakefield looked at the detective with stricken eyes. "My daughter Elizabeth is a straight-A student and a very responsible young lady. Jessica can be a bit hotheaded, but she would never—*never*—put us through something like this." Mrs. Wakefield took a deep breath and then plowed on as Mr. Wakefield jumped in.

Suddenly, both of them were talking at once.

". . . editor-in-chief . . ."

". . . excels in dance . . ."

". . . made her bed every morning since she was five . . ."

". . . I know my children . . . and . . ."

". . . as a father, I'm pretty tuned in and . . ."

Steven's head swiveled back and forth as he listened to his parents desperately trying to convince the police detective that neither Jessica nor Elizabeth would ever run away.

Finally, the detective held up his hands. "Hold it. Hold it," he said. "Nine parents out of ten who report their children as missing say their child wasn't the type to run away. And you know what? Most of the time, we're looking at a runaway situation."

Mr. Wakefield blew his breath out in impatience, and Mrs. Wakefield moaned and sat down on the couch with her head in her hands.

Steven felt awful. This was the most horrible thing he had ever been through. He could hardly bear to see his parents so distraught and upset. His mother looked as if she was about to start sobbing.

I'm never going to put them through anything like this, he vowed silently. *I'm never going to be late coming home again. I'm never going to forget to call them. And I'm never going to run away.*

"Look," Mr. Wakefield said angrily. "It doesn't matter whether they ran away, were abducted, or left to run an errand. All we know is that they're missing, and I want every policeman in Sweet Valley to . . ."

"Hold it, Mr. Wakefield," the detective said, interrupting. "I know you're concerned about your girls, but the police have a lot to do, and we can't go chasing after every kid who's gone off without telling their parents where they're going."

"But . . ." Mrs. Wakefield began.

"I'm sure your girls will turn up today. They probably went out to the Christmas carnival or the mall."

"But . . ." Mr. Wakefield began.

"If they're not back in twenty-four hours, we'll start looking. But when kids run away, if they don't want to be found, we don't find 'em."

"They did *not* run away," Mr. Wakefield insisted.

The detective nodded skeptically. "Did you have some kind of argument? Were they upset about anything?"

Mrs. Wakefield's mouth fell open. Then she tightened her lips.

"Well, yes," Mr. Wakefield conceded. "The girls wanted to attend a party. Mrs. Wakefield and I agreed that the party was not appropriate for two twelve-year-olds. So we did have a disagreement, but . . ."

The detective and the officer exchanged a knowing look. "Mr. Wakefield," the detective began, "I've got a couple of kids of my own, and the only thing I can say I know for sure about them is that I never know for sure what they will or won't do. Ten to one, your girls decided to run away without thinking it through. And when they realize that there's no place like home, they'll be back."

"But they didn't run away," Mrs. Wakefield insisted in an angry voice. "Something's happened to them. That woman took them or lured them away or . . ."

"Like I said before," the detective said, interrupting again, "we can't start looking until they've been gone twenty-four hours."

"But they're children!" Mrs. Wakefield shouted.

Mr. Wakefield sighed reluctantly. "Alice, maybe they're right."

Mrs. Wakefield shook her head. "I just can't believe that they would run away."

"They might have gotten up early and gone shopping." He squeezed her hand and took one of Steven's. "Let's not panic yet. OK?"

The detective and the policeman nodded their good-byes and let themselves out the front door.

As soon as it had slammed behind them, Steven went to the downstairs hall closet and got out his jacket.

"Where are you going?" Mrs. Wakefield asked.

"I'm going out for a little while," Steven said. "I thought I'd take a look around the neighborhood."

Mr. Wakefield nodded. "Good idea. I think I'll take a look around, too. We'll meet back here at ten. But don't you disappear on us, too."

"I won't," he promised.

Steven opened the front door and stepped out into the sunlight. As he hurried down the front walk, he remembered that he hadn't eaten any breakfast. But it didn't really matter. He couldn't have eaten anything anyway. There was another huge lump of guilt in his stomach.

If the twins have really run away, it's all my fault, he thought miserably. *If I'd kept my big mouth shut, or told the truth about the party, Jessica and Elizabeth probably would've been allowed to go—and they'd have had no reason to run away.* He felt sick to his stomach as he walked down the sidewalk. *I've got to be the crummiest brother in the whole world.*

*   *   *

"Drive carefully," the doughnut man called as Jessica and Elizabeth began to leave the bakery office.

"We will," Jessica assured him.

"I don't believe this," Elizabeth said as the two girls walked out into the parking lot with the list of deliveries to be made.

Jessica smirked. "It was so easy I almost feel guilty." Then she laughed and began humming the tune to "I Enjoy Being a Girl."

Elizabeth laughed, too. "You're amazing, you know that?" she said. "There's no way I could've thought up a story like that. That part about our purses being snatched on the bus this morning was really too much. I mean, what are the odds that *both* our purses would be snatched on the same bus ride?"

Jessica tossed the keys into the air and caught them. "Frankly, Lizzie, I don't think it was only the story that did it. Our friend the doughnut man seemed to respond pretty well to a few smiles." She flashed Elizabeth the same dazzling smile that had unhinged the doughnut man.

"Hmmm, good point," Elizabeth said. "I'm surprised he can even remember his own name. He really didn't want to let us go without a driver's license, but you completely discombobulated the poor guy."

The girls reached the truck, and Jessica

climbed up in the driver's seat. "All aboard," she said. "How about you hold the map and help me figure out how to get where we're going?"

Elizabeth stood perfectly still. "Um, Jess, there's just one teeny, tiny little problem.

Jessica ran her hand along the dashboard as though admiring its surface. "Hmmm?"

"You don't know how to drive."

Jessica gave Elizabeth a look of derision. "Oh, come on, Lizzie, how hard can it be? If a jerk like Barney Betner can drive, then the two of us for sure ought to be able to figure out how to do it."

Elizabeth sighed wearily and climbed up into the passenger seat. It looked like one of those situations where Jessica would refuse to be swayed. And maybe she had a point. Maybe now that they had grown up, driving ability would come naturally.

Jessica stared at the dashboard. "Hmmm. Let's see. I guess the key goes in here and . . . aha! . . . the key fits perfectly. Now what?"

"I think you turn it."

Jessica turned it. "Nothing's happening."

Elizabeth peered down at the floor. "I think you have to press the gas pedal."

"Which pedal is that?"

"The one on the right."

"What's the one on the left?"

"The brakes, I think."

Jessica nodded. "Okeydokey, I think I know everything I need to know, so let's move out."

Jessica turned the key while stepping on the gas, and the engine started up. Then she threw the gear shift into drive, slammed her foot on the gas, and . . .

Varrooom!

. . . the van shot forward as if it had been fired out of a cannon.

"Slow down!" Elizabeth shouted.

Screeeee!

. . . went the tires as Jessica slammed the brake pedal with her foot.

Elizabeth let out a gasp as she was thrown forward. Fortunately, her seat belt saved her from bonking her head on the dashboard.

She took a few deep breaths to calm herself and looked at her sister. "I don't think you're supposed to floor the gas or the brake. I think you just kind of tap them gently."

"Got it," Jessica said. She stepped on the gas pedal, and the truck jerked forward. In order to slow it down, she tapped the brake again.

The van slowed too much, so Jessica hit the gas again.

Varrooom!

The truck raced a few yards forward, and Jessica turned the wheel.

Screee! went the tires.

Varrooom! went the engine.

Screeee! went the tires again.

Elizabeth groaned and put her hand on her forehead. "I wish I hadn't eaten all those doughnuts," she said mournfully. "This start/stop driving technique is making me carsick."

"If you're going to barf, please try to do it out the window," Jessica advised. "I've got enough to worry about just keeping this thing moving in a straight line."

"Look out!" Elizabeth screamed ten minutes later.

Jessica slammed on the brakes.

Screeech!

"That's the third bicycle we've almost hit," Elizabeth snapped.

Jessica hit the gas.

Varrooom! went the engine.

"Boy, this is harder than it looks," Jessica muttered.

"Take a right! Take a right!" Elizabeth screamed. Then she noticed a child on a skateboard who was crossing against the light. *"No. No. Forget the turn. Stop!"*

Jessica slammed on the brakes.

Screeech! went the tires of Jessica's truck.

Screeech! went the tires of the car behind them as the driver slammed on his brakes to avoid rear-ending their doughnut truck.

The squeal of the tires was quickly followed by five explosive crashing noises.

Blam!

Blam!

Blam!

Blam!

Blam!

"Oops," Jessica said, glancing in the rearview mirror.

"Jessica!" Elizabeth moaned. "You just caused a five-car pileup."

Jessica drew a sharp breath. "Oh, no," she whispered. "Now we're really in trouble. Here comes a policeman."

Elizabeth's head whipped around. "Uh-oh. We don't have a driver's license. No ID, either."

"What do you think they'll do to us?" Jessica asked fearfully.

Elizabeth wrung her hands. "They might take us downtown and lock us up."

"We're too young to go to jail," Jessica protested.

Elizabeth raised an eyebrow at her sister. "I know that and you know that. But what do you think that policeman is going to say when we tell him we're twelve?"

Jessica glanced once more at the approaching policeman. "Let's split up," she suggested.

Elizabeth's heart began to beat wildly. "Split up?"

"Think about it, Lizzie. He can't follow two of us at once, and we'll have a better chance of getting away if we go in two different directions. You head for South Boulevard and then double back to the corner of Johnson Street. I'll take the road that goes around the library and meet you behind the alley fence at the corner of Johnson. Got it?"

The policeman was getting nearer now. Taking deep breaths, Elizabeth put her hand on the door handle and watched his approach in the mirror that was mounted on the passenger side of the truck.

"Now!" Jessica commanded.

Elizabeth wrenched open the door, jumped out of the truck, and took off like a shot. She had always been a fast runner, and when she lowered her head and pushed into overdrive, she knew she could cover more ground than most grown-ups.

"Hey! Stop!" she heard the policeman shout as she ran across the street and along the sidewalk. Elizabeth never slowed and never looked back. She was glad that the policeman was chasing her and not Jessica. Her sister couldn't run too fast in her mother's heels.

The footsteps behind Elizabeth were rapid and

light, but after a few minutes they began to slow. Elizabeth rounded another corner and headed east on South Boulevard. Then she crossed the street, turned, and began walking west on the sidewalk, affecting an unhurried and unconcerned air.

The policeman came hurtling around the corner on the other side of the street and continued running east along the sidewalk.

Elizabeth smiled. He was so busy looking for a woman who was running like mad that he didn't pay any attention to the young woman on the other side of the street—strolling along as if she had nothing to fear at all.

Steven hurried up Main Street with his hands shoved deep down into his pockets. He had checked the newsstand, the park, the diner, and the pharmacy.

Nobody had seen the twins all morning.

He sighed heavily. The next logical place to look was the mall.

As he walked, the noise of a crowd attracted his attention. There was a lot of yelling going on, and he could hear a policeman's whistle. Whatever was happening, it was right around the corner.

Steven quickly turned the corner and managed to wriggle through the crowd. When he reached the front, his jaw dropped. *There she is!* he thought as he caught a glimpse of that familiar blond lady before she disappeared around the corner of the road that circled the library.

"Perfect timing, Steven." Her voice echoed in his memory.

His heart began to pound as the questions he'd asked himself earlier that morning replayed in his mind. How had she known him? And what did she know about Jessica and Elizabeth?

Steven began to run. Steven was one of the best runners at Sweet Valley High, but she had too much of a head start. If he cut across South Boulevard, though, he could probably intercept her where the library road dead-ended into an alley at the corner of Sierra.

He sprinted forward, crossing the street and angling across the next intersection. He pounded down the next block, gaining more and more speed. As he approached the corner of South Boulevard and Johnson, he leaned into the curve and . . .

"Yeooow!" He hurtled past someone, missing her by inches.

"Yeooow!" he yelled again as that someone grabbed the back of his jacket and yanked him backward. Then that someone pulled him down a side street and into an alley behind a high fence.

"*Cut it out! What do you want? HELP!*" he managed to yell in terror before a hand closed over his mouth.

Fourteen

Steven thrashed this way and that. But the hand that held his jacket never relaxed.

"Cut it out," a female voice said.

Steven jerked forward, but the hand yanked him backward again, throwing him off balance.

"Oops!" the female voice exclaimed as Steven fell.

"Ouch!" Steven yelled as his behind hit the pavement.

He looked up and saw a familiar face bending over him. "Are you all right?" she asked.

Steven's mouth opened, but he was too surprised to get any words out. It was the blond lady. The one who had been in their house, only now she . . .

Steven put his hand over his forehead, suddenly

feeling incredibly dizzy. Ten seconds ago he had seen this woman running around in his mother's black jumpsuit, the same thing she had on this morning. So what was she doing in his mom's blue skirt and jacket? When had she had time to change?

Steven looked up at the woman again and scowled as hard as he could, trying to look intimidating—not an easy thing to do when you're sprawled on the pavement of a dirty alley. Shakily, he stood up. "What are you doing in my mom's clothes?" he demanded. "And what have you done with my sisters?"

A smile played around the corners of the lady's mouth. But before she could answer, they heard the sound of footsteps running in their direction from the opposite end of the alley.

The blond lady's shoulders sagged as if she was relieved. "Wow!" said another female voice. "Take it from me, don't ever try the hundred-yard dash in pumps. I thought I'd never get here." Then she laughed. "Well, well, well. Look who's here. How was the party, Steven?"

Steven whirled around and gasped. "There are two of you?"

Both of the women laughed. "You ought to be used to it by now," the one in the black jumpsuit said in a teasing tone.

"He wanted to know what we had done with his sisters," the lady in blue said.

The one in black cocked an eyebrow at him. "What's it worth to you to know?"

Both women laughed hysterically.

Steven frowned. He couldn't shake the feeling that he knew these women from somewhere. Maybe it was the way they spoke—or laughed— or teased him.

It was crazy. It was insane. It was . . .

The lady in blue stopped laughing first and gave him a sympathetic look. "I think he's had enough, Jess. No more teasing. OK?"

Jess!

Suddenly, Steven felt as if everything were closing in around him—as if he were in a dark tunnel with only a pinpoint of light shining miles away. His knees buckled and he felt himself falling.

"Catch him, Lizzie!" he heard.

A pair of strong arms hooked him under the armpits and kept him from hitting the pavement again. "Got him."

The next thing Steven knew, he was sitting on top of a crate, and someone was shoving his head down between his knees.

"Steven?" a soft, sympathetic voice said. "Are you OK?"

Steven shook his head back and forth, trying to clear it. "I'm sick," he said. "I'm sick in the head."

"No, you're not."

"Yes, I am. I think you'd better take me to the nut hospital. I'm out of my mind."

"There's nothing wrong with your mind," one of them insisted.

"I think *that* might be stretching it, Lizzie. Let's not go overboard," the other one said with a giggle.

"It can't be," Steven moaned. "It just can't be."

He sat up and stared in horror at the two lovely faces that were staring back at him. "Elizabeth?" he whispered. "Jessica?"

Both women nodded.

Steven closed his eyes and groaned again. "It's a dream," he muttered. "A really insane dream."

Two fingers clamped down on the fleshy part of his upper arm and pinched.

"Ouch!" he screamed. His eyes flew open, then narrowed angrily. "Who pinched me?"

The lady in black folded her arms over her chest and smirked. "Still think you're dreaming?"

Steven came up off the crate as if he had been sitting on a hot seat. "I'm getting out of—"

But just then both women grabbed him by the shoulders of his jacket, pulling him back and pushing him down on the crate again.

"Cut it out, Steven. We need your help," the lady in black said.

"Who? . . . What? . . . How? . . ."

"OK, here's the story," the woman in black said briskly. "You know that wishing well at the carnival. Well, we made a wish. We wished we were big."

Steven looked at them in amazement. "What made you do a dumb thing like that?" he shouted in exasperation.

The two women exchanged a glance.

"Maybe it was because a certain person, who shall remain nameless, treated us like rodents because he was a big kid and we weren't," the lady in black suggested.

Steven felt his ears and neck grow hot. He felt so ashamed, he wished he could just crawl into the apple crate and never come out again. Sure, lots of guys teased their little brothers and sisters, but none of them had made their siblings so unhappy that they had wished themselves into a whole other generation. "I'm sorry," he said hoarsely.

Elizabeth put her hand around his shoulder. "It wasn't just you, Steven. It was Mom and Dad, too. And the salesclerk at the bookstore."

"And the makeup consultant at Kendall's."

"Huh?" Steven and Elizabeth said together.

"Long story," Jessica said.

Steven's head was spinning. "OK, OK. So what exactly am I supposed to tell Mom and Dad?"

"Don't tell them anything," Elizabeth said. "Not yet."

He looked at them in bewilderment. "Where are you going to sleep? What are you going to eat? What are you going to do?"

"Yeah, Liz. Where *are* we going to sleep? And where *are* we going to eat? And speaking of eating . . . I'm hungry right now."

Elizabeth nodded and smiled. "Me, too. Hard to believe, isn't it? When I was twelve, three doughnuts would have filled me up for the whole day."

"Well, I guess since we're bigger, we need to eat more. Cool, huh?" Jessica said.

Elizabeth turned to Steven. "Have you got any money?"

Steven reached into his pocket and pulled out several bills. "Here. Take it all."

Elizabeth quickly counted the bills. "Thanks. We'll pay this back as soon as we can. In the meantime, you go home. Try to sneak our sleeping bags into the room over the garage. Also, towels, soap, toothbrushes, and toothpaste. Sneak a couple of Dad's shirts out of his drawer. We can sleep in those. I'm afraid if you take two of Mom's nightgowns, she'll notice."

Steven stared at Elizabeth in amazement. She had always been the practical, get-the-job-done kid in the family, but this was unbelievable.

She'd been grown up for less than a day, and already she was practically the most efficient adult he'd ever met.

"Since we don't know how long this is going to last," Elizabeth continued, "we'd better figure out how we're going to cope."

"I don't know about you," Jessica said, sitting down on the crate and wincing as she eased her feet out of Mrs. Wakefield's black pumps, "but I can't cope with anything until I get something to eat. Where can we get a good, square, well-balanced meal?"

"I'll start with an ice cream sundae. After that, I'll have a piece of triple-layer chocolate cake with a side order of vanilla pudding. And for dessert I'll have a fudge brownie," Jessica finished, smiling as she handed the waitress her menu.

"*That's* what you call a well-balanced meal?" Elizabeth commented.

"Hey, this is the upside of adulthood. Nobody can tell us what to eat. We can order anything we want."

Elizabeth smiled at the waitress and closed her menu. "I'll have two scrambled eggs, toast, and a fruit salad."

The waitress made a little notation on her pad and threw an envious look at Jessica. "How does she stay so thin eating all those sweets?"

"Exercise," Jessica answered promptly. "I ran this morning."

The waitress hurried away to turn in their order, and Elizabeth looked around the coffee shop. "I can't believe it's only ten. I feel like I've lived a lifetime in the last couple of hours."

She looked around the restaurant. A lady slid out of the booth opposite the girls, picked up her purse, coat, and shopping bags full of Christmas packages, and started toward the exit.

"Excuse me," Elizabeth called after her.

The lady turned. "Yes?"

"You left your paper."

The lady smiled. "Thank you for telling me, but I've finished reading it."

"Do you mind if I take it?"

"Not at all."

"Thanks a lot," Elizabeth said. She leaned out and snatched the newspaper. She read the index eagerly.

"What are you doing?" Jessica asked her.

Elizabeth located section B and turned to page five. "I'm checking out the job market."

"You mean jobs for us?"

"That's right," Elizabeth replied, scanning the want ads. "The three of us can't live on Steven's allowance forever."

*   *   *

"No one has seen them?" Mrs. Wakefield asked her husband soon after he arrived back home on Friday morning. Her face was tense and worried.

Mr. Wakefield removed his jacket and draped it over the back of one of the kitchen chairs. "Alice, let's try to stay calm. The girls might have gotten up early and gone shopping." His tone of voice was reassuring and collected, but his own face was white, and his lips formed a grim line.

Steven bit his tongue. It was horrible not being able to tell his parents that Elizabeth and Jessica were safe. But it would be more horrible if they knew the truth—they'd really freak out to know their twelve-year-old daughters were now college-age.

Steven eyed his father. He wasn't absolutely sure, but he thought that Jessica and Elizabeth were taller than he was. It would be pretty tough on his dad to have to look *up* to yell at the twins.

"I'm calling Mrs. Sutton," Mrs. Wakefield said, reaching for the phone book. "And if she doesn't have any information, I'm going to call every single one of Elizabeth's and Jessica's friends."

Mr. Wakefield put his arm around her shoulder. "Give me some of the names. I'll call from the phone in my den."

While his parents went over the list of the

girls' friends, Steven stealthily withdrew from the kitchen and hurried up the stairs. He had a lot to do. And it wasn't going to be easy.

His mother was settling into the kitchen for a long siege. And the sliding glass doors that formed the back wall of the kitchen meant she had a clear view of the garage and the entrance to the steps that led to the room above.

In fact, now that he thought about it, the living room had sliding glass doors that faced the backyard and garage, too.

So how was he going to get everything moved to the garage without being seen?

"You want me to *what*?"

"I want you to ring the doorbell and run away," Steven repeated.

"Are you out of your mind?" Joe asked. "I'm in high school, remember? I gave up recreational doorbell ringing when I was in fifth grade."

"That's OK. I know your skills are a little rusty, but I trust you anyway," Steven said reassuringly.

Joe laughed and leaned against the frame of the Howells' front door. "Can you at least tell me why I should do this for you?"

Steven shook his head. "Sorry, it's a little hard to get into. But if you're really my friend, you'll help me."

Joe frowned and let out a sigh. "Well—OK. Let me get my jacket. But I can't help you too long. We're still cleaning up from the party, and Janet's flown the coop. If I don't get things in order before this afternoon, my father will make my life miserable."

"Ready?" Steven whispered.

"Ready," Joe answered.

"OK, figure on five-minute intervals . . . starting . . ." Steven looked at his watch ". . . *now!*"

Steven hurried up the driveway that led along the side of the house. At the edge of the drive, he had stacked the sleeping bags, towels, shirts, toiletries, and other provisions he thought the twins might need.

He stepped over the pile and edged his way toward the corner of the house, holding a mirror he had taken off Jessica's bureau. By angling the handheld mirror, he could see the reflection of his mother talking on the phone in the kitchen. She was facing the backyard and the garage.

Dingdong!

Even from outside, Steven could hear the faint ring of the doorbell.

Just as he had hoped, Mrs. Wakefield said something quickly into the phone, hung up the receiver, and left the kitchen.

It was time to move and move fast. Sticking

the mirror into his back pocket, Steven swiveled around. He grabbed a sleeping bag in each hand and then ran for the garage, opening the little door that led to the garage stairwell with his foot. Quick as lightning, he slipped inside the door and let it close behind him with a soft thud.

He ran up the stairs, opened the door to the room above the garage, and deposited the sleeping bags on the floor.

Then he ran back down the stairs and waited behind the door. *So far so good.* He looked at his watch. Two minutes before the next run.

He began to breathe slowly, pacing his wind, as the track coach had taught him. Inhale. Exhale. Inhale. Exhale.

Steven closed his eyes and counted out the seconds. "Fifty-five, fifty-six, fifty-seven, fifty-eight, fifty-nine, and . . ."

Steven burst out the door, crossed the yard in a matter of seconds, and grabbed the two small suitcases he had packed. As in a relay race, he scooped them up and pivoted without ever coming to a stop.

Sweat was pouring down his forehead by the time he got up to the garage room again. He threw the suitcases inside and then thundered down the steps. One more trip and he was home free.

*   *   *

Ten minutes later, Steven ran up the front steps of the Wakefields' house just as Joe came running down.

He could hear two sets of footsteps coming toward the front door. Two sets of angry footsteps.

Joe dove headfirst over the hedge that separated the Wakefields' yard from the neighbors', and Steven turned his back toward the door two seconds before it was yanked open.

". . . And I mean *stay away!*" Steven yelled.

"What's going on?" his father demanded. "Who keeps ringing the doorbell?"

Steven shook his head and twisted his face into an expression of disgust. "Just some little kids with nothing better to do."

"Kids from the neighborhood?" Mrs. Wakefield asked.

"Maybe," Steven said. "They looked like they were in about the fifth grade."

From behind the hedge there was a muffled snort of laughter.

"Do your mother and me a favor. Stand out here for a little while and make sure they don't do it again." Mr. Wakefield ran a hand over his face. "We're trying to track down the girls, and we don't want to be interrupted every five minutes by the doorbell."

"Sure," Steven said with a nod. "I'll make sure it doesn't happen again."

The door shut behind him, and Steven sat down on the top step. Now that it was over, his legs were wobbling, and he realized his heart was pounding.

Now all he had to do was sneak the girls in tonight after dark.

Fifteen

"I wish I'd remembered to grab a couple of Mom's lipsticks," Jessica said wistfully as she examined her reflection in the window of the bus. *And a little blush would do wonders,* she decided. "Maybe we should buy some makeup. Look at those shops." She pointed toward a row of old-fashioned Victorian-cottage shops that were decorated for Christmas. "There's the Nature's Way Beauty Shop. I'll bet we could get some really great cosmetics in there."

Elizabeth shook her head. "Forget it, Jessica. It's a job interview, not a beauty pageant. Besides, we don't have time. We have to get to the Zippy Personnel Temp Service before noon so that we can get the twenty-dollar signing bonus. They must really be desperate for help. I guess a lot of people take days off around Christmastime."

"Think they'll have any jobs for actresses?" Jessica asked in a hopeful voice.

Elizabeth shook her head. "I doubt it."

"Rock star?"

Elizabeth laughed.

"Model, at least?"

Elizabeth checked the newspaper one more time. "According to the ad, the Zippy Personnel Temp Service has immediate placement for file clerks and receptionists." She looked out the bus window and pulled the stop cord.

Jessica frowned in confusion as the bus pulled to a stop in front of the Sweet Valley Mall. "I thought you said we didn't have time to shop."

"We don't," Elizabeth replied. "The Zippy Personnel Temp Service is in the office tower that's attached to the mall."

"Neat," Jessica said happily. "I like the Zippy Personnel Temp Service already."

"Elizabeth, look!" Jessica grabbed Elizabeth's sleeve and pointed. It was all Jessica could do not to let out a gleeful shriek when she saw Janet Howell, Lila Fowler, Ellen Riteman, Tamara Chase, Grace Oliver, Betsy Gordon, and Mandy Miller—practically the whole Unicorn Club.

They were looking in the window of an elegant shop, where a mannequin modeled a long sequined evening gown.

"Come on," Jessica whispered, tugging at Elizabeth's arm.

"Where are we going?" Elizabeth protested. "Jess, we don't have much—"

"It'll only take a second," Jessica assured her. "Just play along with me. It'll be fun."

She and Elizabeth crept up behind the group of Unicorns, towering over them.

"Can you believe she danced with Denny *twice*?" Janet was saying. "I was so mad I wanted to scream."

"If it had been my party, I would have asked her to leave," Ellen Riteman said in a nasty voice.

"Well, I *would* have, but Joe wouldn't let me," Janet said.

Jessica listened with avid interest. Denny Jacobson was Janet's boyfriend, and Janet was a very jealous kind of girl. Jessica desperately wanted to know who had dared to dance with Denny twice.

"Janet," Lila whispered. "I think those ladies behind us are listening."

Janet looked back over her shoulder and frowned at Jessica.

Jessica immediately lifted her gaze to the window and pretended to be looking at the dress. "Oh, Tiffany," she said to Elizabeth in a deep, actressy voice. "It's perfect. Just what I need for Johnny Buck's Christmas party."

Out of the corner of her eye, Jessica could see that Janet was no longer frowning. She was gawking. And so were the other Unicorns, for that matter.

"Oh, are you going to his party again this year?" Elizabeth responded in a deep, affected voice. "I would have thought that being a supermodel would keep you pretty busy during the Christmas season. All those holiday layouts to shoot."

"Well, I *am* busy, of course," Jessica said dismissively. "But you know how it is. If Johnny asks me to go, I just hate to say no. He's always so sweet to me."

The Unicorns were staring at Jessica and Elizabeth with big, bulging eyes.

Janet cleared her throat. "Excuse me. Did I hear you say you knew Johnny Buck?"

Jessica looked at the girls as if she were just noticing them. She lifted her eyebrows haughtily and stared down her nose at Janet. "Yes, dear, Johnny Buck and I have been friends for years."

"How did you get to be a supermodel?" Janet asked in a breathless tone. "I would like to be a supermodel when I grow up."

"We both would," Lila added. "Do you have any tips for us?"

Jessica appeared to give the question a great deal of thought. "Well," she said after a long pause. "I suppose I would advise that you think positive and don't give up. Lots of supermodels start life as very *plain* little girls."

Janet's and Lila's faces fell, and Jessica gave them a sweet, vaguely sympathetic smile. "Come on, Tiffany. We're late for lunch with our agents."

Jessica lifted her chin and glided gracefully away, leaning slightly backward like a runway model, luxuriating in the thought that Janet and Lila were watching her with envious eyes.

But for some reason, it didn't make her feel all that great. In fact, now that she stopped to think about it, she felt a little sad. It would have been much more fun to have found out who had the nerve to dance with Denny Jacobson at Janet's party.

Beside her, Elizabeth let out an unhappy sigh.

"What's the matter?" Jessica asked.

"It's strange not to be recognized," Elizabeth said slowly. "In a way, it's like Elizabeth and Jessica Wakefield died."

"Yuck, Elizabeth. What a morbid thing to say!" Jessica exclaimed.

"Didn't you feel just a little bit like a ghost back there," Elizabeth pressed.

Jessica's sagging spirits sank even deeper.

"If we're not Jessica and Elizabeth Wakefield anymore, who are we?"

Elizabeth hesitated. "Elizabeth and Jessica Smith," she replied finally. "At least that's what we say if anybody asks."

Ms. Peters, an agent at the Zippy Personnel Temp Service, read over Elizabeth's application and lifted an eyebrow in surprise. "You've had no work experience at all, Ms. Smith?"

"That's right," Elizabeth said. "No professional experience, that is. But I have worked very hard on the *Sixers*, my school newspaper. In fact, I'm the one who started the paper."

Ms. Peters cleared her throat. "You mean your old school newspaper," she clarified. "The *Sixers* is a sixth-grade newspaper at Sweet Valley Middle School."

Elizabeth's heart skipped a beat. "You're right," she said with a laugh. "Of course, I'm long out of sixth grade. I'm in the, ahhhh . . ." Her mind went blank. She wasn't sure how old she was. "Well, I'm sure not in the sixth grade," she joked lamely. "I guess I should have said I worked on the *Sixers* a long time ago."

Ms. Peters gave her a thin smile. "My niece attends Sweet Valley Middle School. It was my understanding that the *Sixers* was begun this year."

"It was," Elizabeth agreed immediately.

"Then how could you have worked on it?"

"Well . . . ahhh . . . I didn't go to middle school in California. I went to middle school in . . . ahhhh . . . Kansas. And our sixth-grade newspaper was called the *Sixers*. When I moved to Sweet Valley, I mentioned it to a young cousin of mine at Sweet Valley Middle School, and she mentioned it to some of her friends and . . . ummm . . . that's how they got the idea to have a sixth-grade paper called the *Sixers*." Elizabeth's heart was racing, and she was having a hard time controlling her breathing.

Ms. Peters smiled warmly. "How nice. The staff of the *Sixers* owes a debt to you."

Elizabeth blushed. "It's not really that big a deal."

"Now, now," Ms. Peters said in a rallying voice. "Modesty is fine, but there's no sense in hiding your light under a bushel during a job interview." She picked up a little deck of index cards and began searching through them. "I had a call this morning from a publishing company and . . . *aha!*" She pulled a card from the deck. "This is your lucky day."

"It is?"

"Sweet Valley Publishing needs a receptionist." She picked up a pen and began scribbling on a pad. "Here's the address. They're located quite near here." She tore the paper off the pad and handed it to Elizabeth, along with a crisp twenty-dollar bill.

Elizabeth stared down at the money and bit her lip.

"Is there something wrong?"

"Well, about the money—that is, what if . . . something . . . some unforeseen circumstance . . . prevents me from being able to go back on Monday? Am I supposed to return this?"

"Don't worry," Ms. Peters said reassuringly. "We offer these bonuses to attract new personnel. If things don't work out, our attitude is that we at least owe you for the time you spent talking to us."

"Thank you," Elizabeth said, folding the bill and tucking it into her pocket. "I'll do the best job I can."

"Ms. Smith, are you uncomfortable?" Mr. Gonzales asked Jessica during her interview.

"No," Jessica said, idly twirling a piece of her hair around her finger. "Why do you ask?"

"I suppose because it is not customary to sit cross-legged in a chair while conducting business." His voice was sharp and bossy, and he sort of reminded Jessica of Mr. Clark, the principal at Sweet Valley Middle School.

Jessica straightened her legs and sat up in her

chair. This job-interview business was taking forever. But she guessed it was worth it if she got to keep the crisp twenty-dollar bill in her pocket.

"Now, then," Mr. Gonzales continued, "let's discuss what you would like to do."

"Do you have any modeling assignments?" Jessica asked in a hopeful voice.

Mr. Gonzales gave her another frown. "I'm afraid not," he answered dryly. "But I have a lot of requests for a file clerk."

Jessica slumped down in her chair a little. *Gag*, she thought.

"Now, then," Mr. Gonzales said again. "all I need to determine is, what field do you wish to work in?"

"I don't know," Jessica responded. "What field would you suggest?"

"Hmmm. How about finance?"

Jessica gave him a blank look. She wasn't even sure what that meant.

"Real estate?"

Jessica shook her head.

"Investments? . . . Law? . . . Hotel and restaurant management?"

Jessica was getting a headache from shaking her head back and forth.

"Fashion?" Mr. Gonzales suggested in exasperation.

Jessica sat straight up in her seat. "Bingo!"

Sixteen

Jessica stared out the bus window on her way to work. It felt weird to be by herself, and she wished that she and Elizabeth were going to be working at the same place.

But Elizabeth had been all excited about going to work for a publisher, and she had stopped outside the Zippy office only long enough to wish Jessica good luck and arrange to meet her back at the diner after work.

Jessica felt a little nervous flutter in her stomach. She couldn't believe she was actually going to work, just like a grown-up. And she was going to a fashion company. She sat up a little straighter and pretended that she was a model on her way to an assignment.

She tossed her blond hair off her shoulders

and rolled her head around on her neck, as if she were posing for a camera. She opened her eyes wide, lifted one shoulder, and peered backwards over it.

Much to her embarrassment, she found herself staring into the eyes of the man who sat behind her.

He gave her a big smile and chuckled. "Have you got a crick in your neck?"

Jessica blushed a fiery red. "I . . . ah . . . ahhh . . . no. This is how I unwind before I go to work."

"It's a little late in the day to be on your way to work, isn't it?"

He's only teasing, Jessica told herself, but she felt stupid anyway. She definitely wasn't in the mood to be teased, not when she was about to start her first day at work. She tossed her head haughtily. "It's not late for a supermodel," she said in her actressy voice.

The man raised his eyebrows. "Are you a supermodel?"

"Yes, I am. And I'm on my way to a shoot."

"Gosh. I never realized that supermodels got around town on the bus."

"My limo broke down, you see," she explained, "so I got on the bus."

"That's really big of you," the man said. "Very professional."

He was clearly waiting for Jessica to respond

again, but Jessica's attention was focused on the buildings that were whizzing past the window. When she saw the number eleven thirty-three, she knew she was only a few buildings away from her destination—Y&C Clothing. She was just about to pull the stop cord, but the man behind her pulled it first.

"This is my stop," he said with a smile. "It was nice talking to you."

Jessica gave him a radiant supermodel smile. "It was nice talking to you. And this is my stop, too."

The man politely stepped aside and let Jessica exit the bus ahead of him.

"Bye," she said, walking up the sidewalk.

The man fell into step beside her.

"Guess we're going in the same direction," she chirped.

"Looks like it," he agreed.

When she reached number eleven sixty, she veered toward the door.

The man veered with her and also went into the building. Jessica started to get a little nervous. Maybe this guy was following her.

She was just about to demand an explanation when the receptionist gave the man a big smile. "Hi, Chuck. How did the shoot go?"

That's when Jessica noticed that he had a couple of cameras slung over his shoulder.

"It went fine," he said.

"You work here?" she asked in a faint voice.

Chuck nodded. "I'm the staff photographer for Y and C Clothing, Inc."

Jessica's face felt as if it were on fire. *Why does he have to be the staff photographer, of all things?*

A woman dressed in black from head to toe came bearing down on Jessica, frowning deeply. "Are you Ms. Smith?" she asked in an impatient voice.

"Yes," Jessica squeaked.

"You're late," the woman barked.

"I'm . . . sorry . . ." Jessica stuttered in confusion. "But I came by bus and . . ."

"Ms. Smith's personal vehicle broke down," Chuck said, the corners of his mouth twitching slightly. "I think we should be glad she cared enough about the job to take the bus."

Jessica wished the earth would just open up so she could fall in and never be seen again. *He's making fun of me,* she thought with dismay.

"Very well, very well," the woman said in a grudging tone. "It doesn't matter now. I'm Ms. Cook, the clerical-staff supervisor. Come with me. I've got at least three or four hours of filing for you to do."

"Organize the files in alphabetical order first," Ms. Cook began. "Then check the numerical designation on the back tab. If the first four digits correspond to the first four digits of the preceding file, then combine the contents of the two files in a new file and put it in this stack here. Then take the two empty file folders, draw a line through the first eight digits, and refile them in alphabetical *and* numerical order. Any questions? No? Fine."

The next instant, Ms. Cook was gone.

Jessica stood in the middle of the file room with her mouth hanging open.

She looked helplessly around the room. There were stacks of files everywhere. Probably a thousand file folders.

And they all looked like a mess.

"LMNOP," Jessica muttered. She was sitting on the floor in the file room with a huge stack of files in her lap. Putting them in alphabetical order was taking a long time. Once she got past the letter J in the alphabet, she had to start from the very beginning in order to remember the order of the rest of the letters.

She picked up a new file. "ABCDEF . . ." she began, muttering under her breath.

When the file was in the right place, she slumped down and sighed. This was the most incredibly boring thing she had ever done in her whole life.

Being a grown-up wasn't so great after all. Sure, there weren't any teachers or parents around. But who needed parents and teachers when you had somebody like Ms. Cook breathing down your neck?

Ms. Cook was the bossiest person she had ever met. She was bossier than Janet Howell and Mr. Clark put together.

She had come in three times already to supervise Jessica. And every time, she told Jessica that she was doing it all wrong and made her start all over again.

Just as she picked up a new file, Jessica heard a man shouting in the next room. "I thought I made myself clear. Ms. Cook, how many times do I have to fill out a request form for office supplies?"

"I'm sorry, Mr. Ferguson, I'll try to . . ."

Jessica tiptoed to the doorway and peeked around. A man with a bald head and red face shook his finger at Ms. Cook. "You'll have to do better than *try*, Ms. Cook. If I don't get my supplies by three o'clock today, I'm going to be really angry."

He's angry enough now, Jessica thought. *I'd hate to see him get "really angry."*

Jessica darted back into the file room and bit her lip thoughtfully. Ms. Cook seemed so bossy herself that it was hard to believe that somebody actually had the nerve to boss *her* around.

"Mr. Ferguson," she heard another female voice say in an imperious tone. "What is the meaning of this report? I asked you to analyze our sales by units sold, not gross price points."

"Now, Ms. Thompson," Mr. Ferguson said in a completely different voice than the one he had used with Ms. Cook. "I haven't quite finished that . . ."

"I asked for it a week ago," Ms. Thompson said impatiently. "And if I don't get that report on my desk by nine o'clock tomorrow morning . . ."

Jessica put her hands over her ears. This was awful. It was like everybody in the whole company spent their day bossing or being bossed.

She closed her eyes and imagined herself as the top executive of Y&C Clothing, Inc. Nobody would try bossing her. She could do whatever she wanted and not get into trouble with anybody.

A letter slid out of the file in her hand, and Jessica bent over to retrieve it. "Dear Chief Executive Officer of Y&C Clothing, Inc," it read. "As a major stockholder of Y&C, I am writing to express my profound disappointment in last quarter's earnings. If the next quarter does not prove more profitable, I will strongly consider selling my stock short, thereby removing my

financial support of what is clearly a misman-
aged and poorly run company. Very truly yours,
Beverly Madison, stockholder."

Jessica sat down on the floor and sighed.
Maybe there was no such thing as an unbossable
position.

Ms. Cook came trotting in and looked quickly
through the stack Jessica had made. She made a
little impatient clicking sound and shook her
head. "No! No! No! No!" she said irritably. Then
she sighed heavily. "Leave the filing," she
snapped. "It's clearly too difficult for you." She
thrust some handwritten notes into Jessica's
hand and then guided her by the elbow into the
next room. "Type these notes, and I'll be back for
them in twenty minutes." She pointed to a desk
with a computer terminal.

"But I don't know how to use a computer,"
Jessica protested in small voice. Unfortunately,
Ms. Cook had already left.

Jessica turned her attention to the keypad, de-
liberated for a moment or two, then pushed a
button.

The screen went black, and the system let out
a series of electronic squawks and beeps.

"Ms. Smith!" a voice thundered from the next
room. *"What have you done to our computer system?"*

Jessica felt tears begin to trickle down her

cheeks. She had no idea what she had done to the computer system. All she knew was that the whole job business was horrible, awful, icky, and boring.

Why did she make that stupid wish? Why? Life had been so much simpler when she was twelve.

Seventeen

Ring! Ring!

"Sweet Valley Publishing. Happy Holidays."

"Connect me with Robert Pitt," a deep voice commanded.

"One moment, *please*," Elizabeth replied, stressing the world *please*. Adults seemed to have a really hard time saying that word—not to mention "thank you."

She pushed the red hold button and then glanced at her list of intercom numbers. Patterson . . . Pell . . . Peters . . . Post . . . *Hmmmm*, Elizabeth thought. Where was Pitt?

She opened the desk drawer and rummaged around. The supervisor had said something about an addition to the phone list. Maybe Mr. Pitt's intercom number was on that list.

Ring! Ring!
Line Two lit up.
Ring! Ring!
Elizabeth punched the bright button. "Sweet Valley Publishing. Happy Holidays."

"Could you tell me who's in charge of advertising for the mass-market line?"

"Well, you see, I'm a temp," Elizabeth explained, "and I haven't met everybody who works here yet. It's a pretty big place and . . ."

Ring! Ring! went Line Three.

". . . I'm not sure who that would be," Elizabeth finished.

"Could you ask somebody while I hold?" Line Two requested.

Ring! Ring! went Line Three again.

Elizabeth cast an eye around the huge, deserted outer office. She would be happy to ask somebody, but she hadn't seen anybody in at least fifteen minutes. "Maybe it would be better if I took your name and number and . . ."

Ring! Ring! Line Three rang again.

"Aren't you going to answer that?" a man snapped as he whizzed into the lobby from an inner office.

"I'm sorry," Elizabeth sputtered in confusion. "Could you please tell me who's in charge of . . ."

But the man was moving so fast, he never

even paused before he disappeared through another door.

"Hold on, please," Elizabeth told Line Two before answering Line Three. "Sweet Valley Publishing. Happy Holidays."

"I'm waiting to talk to Pitt," Line Three practically shouted. "Are you going to leave me on hold all day?"

"I'm . . . sorry . . . I thought you were on Line One." Elizabeth quickly pushed the hold button again and resumed her search for the addition to the phone list.

"Who's on Line One?" a voice bellowed from an inner office.

Elizabeth didn't know whether that person wanted her to shout back an answer or not. Not that it really mattered—she had no idea who was on Line One.

Zzzaaattt! went her intercom.

She pressed the intercom button. "Reception. Elizabeth speaking."

"Is my lunch here yet?" a brisk voice inquired.

"No, sir," Elizabeth replied. "No one's delivered anyone's lunch."

"Well, call me as soon as it gets here." *Click!*

Elizabeth sighed wearily. *That's going to be tough to do if you don't tell me your name,* Elizabeth thought. She took a deep breath and stared at the phone. Three lines were lit and blinking, and now she couldn't remember who was on what line and what it was they wanted.

"Excuse me, miss."

Elizabeth looked up and saw a deliveryman wearing a deli apron and a paper hat. He plopped a large cardboard box full of food on her desk and plucked the ticket off the side. "Two ham-and-cheese sandwiches on rye," he read. "Four turkey clubs. Three yogurts. Two chef salads. And twelve bottles of sparkling water. That'll be thirty-two dollars and twenty-eight cents."

"Who is it for?" Elizabeth asked.

The deliveryman checked his ticket. "Hmmm. It's hard to read, but it looks like the person who placed the order was somebody named Pitt."

Elizabeth's heart sank, but she smiled politely. "I've had a little trouble locating Mr. Pitt today, but if you would just have a seat, I'll see what I can do."

The deliveryman looked annoyed. "Don't take too long. This is our busiest time of day. I've got a lot of orders to deliver."

Elizabeth rummaged frantically through the drawer.

Ring! Ring!

Ring! Ring!

Zzzaaattt!

Elizabeth pressed the intercom. "Reception. Elizabeth speaking."

"This is the art department. Would you get us a messenger?"

"Yes," Elizabeth answered. "I'll be happy to if you'll tell me who to call."

"Don't you have the number?" the voice asked irritably.

Elizabeth was close to tears. Why was everybody so cranky? Didn't they understand she was just a temp? Why did they think she could recognize people from the sound of their voice, or locate people whose names weren't even on her list of employees?

"Miss!" the deliveryman barked. "I can't sit here all day."

"I know," Elizabeth began, "but . . ."

"Why don't you just pay me the thirty-two bucks and change and let Pitt pay you back when you find him?"

"I don't have thirty-two bucks and change," Elizabeth protested.

"Miss Smith!" a stern voice behind her said. "What *are* you doing out here?"

Elizabeth turned and saw her supervisor standing behind her and staring at her with a look of deep disapproval.

A lump rose in Elizabeth's throat, and hot tears made her eyes sting. How could things have gone so wrong so fast?

Elizabeth had always been a quick study and a

model of efficiency. Not only capable, but responsible, too. She had never felt daunted by challenges at school.

But the world of adults was nothing but pitfalls and potholes. One opportunity after another to fall short of expectation and fail.

Why did I ever make that stupid wish? she wondered miserably. *If only I could be twelve again.*

"I just don't see any way around it," Mr. Wakefield said to Mrs. Wakefield with a sigh.

"Any way around what?" Steven asked, walking into the kitchen. His parents were sitting side by side at the kitchen table. His father's hand rested over his mother's.

Mr. Wakefield looked exhaustedly up at Steven. "Sit down," he instructed.

Steven pulled out one of the kitchen chairs and sat down. He studied the tense, pale faces of his mother and father.

"I don't want you to panic," Mr. Wakefield said in a reassuring tone. "But your mother and I have called every single person we can think of. No one has seen the girls. I think now we should get in the car and drive around. See if we can spot them somewhere."

Mr. Wakefield stood and crossed to the phone. "Let me call Mr. Porter at his hotel and cancel my meeting."

"Mr. Porter?" Steven said. "The guy who's here from London? I thought you said he was your most important client."

Mr. Wakefield nodded. "He is. But no client is as important as my children." He punched the numbers on the phone. "Hello. Would you connect me with Mr. Porter, please? He's in room three sixty-one."

Steven tried to remember all the things his father had said over the last couple of years about Mr. Porter:

Mr. Porter's business gets my area of the law firm through the lean times.

You can thank Mr. Porter for this one, he had joked last year after he bought Mrs. Wakefield a new car.

And one night, when Mr. Wakefield had come home very late after a long meeting: *Mr. Porter is demanding. But he has a right to be. He's a large employer, which means he's responsible for a lot of livelihoods—including our own.*

Steven's mind was racing. If his dad canceled his important meeting, would Mr. Porter get mad? Would it jeopardize his dad's job? Would it translate into a smaller allowance for him and the girls—that is, assuming they ever turned back into girls?

Steven had a sinking feeling in his chest. If they *didn't* turn back into girls, he was going to need every penny of his allowance. The twins were a pretty good-sized pair of adults, and they looked as though they could probably put away a lot of food.

There was no doubt about it. Their father couldn't afford to disappoint Mr. Porter. "Dad, wait!" Steven blurted out in a panic.

Mr. and Mrs. Wakefield both jumped.

"You don't need to cancel your meeting. Hang up. Quick!"

Mr. Wakefield gave Steven a curious look and replaced the receiver. "Steven," he said slowly, "do you know something about the twins that we don't know?"

Steven swallowed hard.

"Answer your father," Mrs. Wakefield commanded sternly.

"Yes," he said hoarsely. "I do know something."

Mr. Wakefield came back to the table and sat down. He fixed Steven with a terrifying stare. "What?"

The neck of Steven's T-shirt suddenly seemed tight. And the temperature in the kitchen had grown uncomfortably warm. Glancing back and forth between his mother and his father, Steven felt his heart pounding in his chest. He had never seen his parents look so intense.

He opened his mouth and closed it again in

confusion. *If I tell them the truth, they'll just think I'm delirious or something,* he thought.

"Are they at least safe?" Mr. Wakefield asked finally.

Steven let out his breath. That, at least, was a question he could answer. "Yes," he said firmly.

"They're not in any danger?" Mrs. Wakefield pressed.

Steven shook his head.

"Does their disappearance have anything to do with their unhappiness over missing the party?" Mr. Wakefield wanted to know.

Steven nodded.

Mr. Wakefield sat back in his chair and sighed. "Do you know when they're coming back?"

Steven bit his lip. He didn't know how to answer that one. True, the twins would be coming back this evening, but they wouldn't be the twins that his parents were waiting for.

Mr. Wakefield leaned slightly forward. "Steven, I don't know what you may have promised the girls as far as secrecy, but I'm telling you right now that not telling us where we can find your sisters is a far worse offense than breaking a promise to them. Will you tell us where they are?"

Steven shook his head miserably. "I can't," he said softly.

"Then you're grounded," Mr. Wakefield said in an even and neutral voice.

Eighteen

Sitting in a cubicle at Y&C Clothing, Jessica took a few more pieces of paper off the huge stack and put them into the hole puncher. The device made a crunching sound as it bit into the paper.

Jessica removed the paper and put it in a three-ring binder.

She looked at the four-foot stack of paper waiting to have holes punched in it. This was the most boring thing she had ever had to do in her whole life. In fact, it made all that filing she'd done earlier that afternoon seem like a blast.

Of course, it seemed that Ms. Cook had purposely found something boring for her to do. *Here, Ms. Smith,* she'd said in a nasty voice. *I think I've found something that not even you can goof up.*

Jessica felt another wave of humiliation wash over her. Ms. Cook had talked to her as if she were an idiot in front of everybody in the whole company, including Chuck.

Chuck had given her a sympathetic look, but that hadn't made Jessica feel better. In fact, it had made her feel even more ashamed and embarrassed. *My limo broke down.* She shuddered as she remembered her lie. *I'm definitely a far cry from supermodel status at this place,* she thought.

Jessica tried to make the job go faster by putting a thicker stack of paper in the puncher. She stuck the sheets in place and pressed down on the hole puncher. This time it didn't make a crunching noise. It made a muffled thudding noise.

Jessica tried to pull the paper out so she could try again, but the paper wouldn't come out. It was jammed. Once again, she'd goofed up.

Jessica groaned in defeat. *I really can't take much more of this,* she thought, dropping her head into her hands. It was pretty clear that she wasn't ready for the job market. What was going to happen to her? Would she have to spend her whole life sneaking in and out of the garage after dark and eating whatever Steven could manage to sneak out of the kitchen?

Jessica closed her eyes. It had all started with that stupid shopping trip to Kendall's. If she had been able to find something to wear—something sophisticated and suitable for her age—her mother would never have questioned her so closely about the party. And if Mrs. Wakefield hadn't questioned her so closely, she and Elizabeth could have gone to the party instead of the carnival, and none of this would have ever happened.

She picked up a pen and began idly doodling on a yellow tablet. She pictured the tiny jackets, skirts, and trousers that her mother had thought were so unsuitable.

Maybe she had been right. The things had been a little extreme. But what if they were toned down a bit? Say the jackets were decorated with appliqués instead of sequins, and the trousers were made of linen instead of silk?

Her pencil flew over the page as she sketched the outfit that existed only in her imagination. The drawing was good. She had captured the line and movement of the jacket, and the little sketch had a lot of drama and style.

She tore off the page and began moving her pencil over the second sheet, designing a dress for Elizabeth.

"Ms. Smith!"

Jessica jumped and dropped her pad. Loose pages flew out in all directions, covering the floor.

Ms. Cook pointed to the stack of paper that she had given Jessica to put into binders. "You've been sitting here two hours," she said in an enraged voice, "and you've hardly made a dent in this stack."

Jessica saw Mr. Ferguson, Ms. Thompson, several young women, and Chuck standing behind Ms. Cook. They all carried notepads and pens, as if they were ready to have a meeting.

"I told you we needed those binders for our afternoon conference," Ms. Cook sputtered. "*What* have you been doing?"

"Who hired this incompetent woman?" Mr. Ferguson demanded.

Jessica could hardly speak, she was so miserable. Chuck stepped over and put his arm around her shoulders. "Hey. Don't get upset. Even supermodels have their bad days."

That was the last straw. Even though he was trying to be nice, his little joke made her feel even more embarrassed and miserable. "Why are you all being so mean to me?" she yelled. "Hasn't anybody told you guys it's the Christmas season?"

Ms. Cook, Ms. Thompson, and Mr. Ferguson all reared a little, as if the force of Jessica's voice had blown them backward.

"We know it's Christmas," Chuck said in a kind voice. "That's why we're all so uptight. We design clothes for little girls, and our holiday line is not selling well at all. In fact, it's a total flop."

"We have no idea what girls want to wear," Mr. Ferguson said. "And if we don't figure it out before next season, we're going to be out of business."

Jessica regained control of her breath. "Well, why didn't you say so? I can tell you what girls want to wear."

"Don't be ridiculous," Ms. Cook said. "How would you know?"

"I know what girls want because I *am* a . . . I mean, *my niece* is a little girl. She and I went shopping a couple of days ago, and we couldn't find anything that was right for a party."

Ms. Thompson made an impatient noise. "Then you must not have looked very hard. I'm head of design and I know we shipped hundreds of velvet jumpers and lacey-collar blouses to local department stores."

"But girls don't want to wear clothes like that," Jessica argued. "And if you ask me, it seems like you ought to be able to figure that out based on your sales."

Ms. Thompson colored hotly, but before she could say anything else, Chuck whistled. "Wow." He was flipping through some of Jessica's papers. "These designs are terrific."

Ms. Cook snatched one out of his hand, and she and Mr. Ferguson studied it.

"That's what kids want to wear to parties," Jessica said. "They may be young, but that doesn't mean they want to dress like babies."

Ms. Thompson, the head of design, eagerly studied the pages Chuck was handing her. "These are good," she murmured. "Not just good. Great." She shot a look at Jessica. "What's your name again?"

"Jessica. Jessica Smith."

"Come with me," Ms. Thompson barked. "You've just been promoted to Assistant Design Consultant for Y and C Clothing, Inc. We'll call the spring line *The Jessica Collection.*"

Jessica was so overwhelmed she didn't know what to say. "What does Y and C stand for?" she asked feebly.

"Young and Chic," Ms. Thompson replied. "And with your help, maybe we can actually come up with some dresses that deserve the label."

Jessica grinned happily, and Chuck gave her the thumbs-up sign and a wink.

The group moved toward the conference room, and Chuck took her arm, pulling her back a little. "Congratulations on your promotion," he said in an admiring tone.

"Thank you," Jessica said, holding her shoulders importantly.

"I was wondering," Chuck continued, looking down at his hands shyly, "may I take you to dinner tonight to celebrate?"

Jessica nearly fell over. She couldn't believe she was actually being asked out by a good-looking fashion photographer. It was a dream come true.

But the person Jessica really wanted to celebrate her fabulous new career with was Elizabeth.

"I already have plans," she said with a smile. "But maybe some other time."

"Sure." Chuck grinned. "I should have known a supermodel would already have a date."

This time, his teasing didn't embarrass her. It was like a little private joke between the two of them, and it made her laugh.

"Miss Smith, would you please bring your pad and join us in the conference room? We're about to have an editorial meeting, and I would like you to take some notes. Brian will take your place at the reception desk."

Elizabeth nodded and relinquished her seat to a smiling young man in a tie. She grabbed a pad and a couple of pens and hurried to catch up with Ms. Miller, Sweet Valley Publishing's sophisticated senior editor.

Ms. Miller led Elizabeth into a large conference room and motioned her toward one of the two empty chairs that sat side by side.

The other chairs around the table were all occupied by several of the men and women she had seen coming and going through the lobby.

Everyone sat up a little straighter as Ms. Miller took her seat next to Elizabeth and called the meeting to order.

"As you all know," she began, "many of our new books have not sold as well as we had hoped. Sweet Valley Publishing desperately needs another book series for spring publication. A book series for middle-grade girls. I would like to hear your ideas."

A lady in a red dress raised her hand. "According to *Authors and Publishers* magazine, horror is selling very well."

"We have a horror series," someone else said. "And I don't know why, but it hasn't done well."

I'll tell you why, Elizabeth thought as she scribbled on her pad. *Because your horror books are horrible. Who wants to wade through all that blood and gore?*

"What about a skating series?" someone else said.

"There's one already out, and it's snagged a large portion of the market."

"Horses," a man said. "Little girls love horses. What about a series about riding? I know that there is already a line of horse books on the market. But there's always room for one more, right?"

Wrong, Elizabeth thought. She loved the horse series that was already out, and she knew she wouldn't be interested in reading any imitations.

As more ideas were discussed, Elizabeth wrote them down on her pad. She wished she could do more than take notes. It was so exciting to be part of a real editorial discussion. It was exactly the kind of thing she had always imagined herself doing.

"More and more girls are taking to the ice," one of the editors was saying. "I think there's definitely room for another skating series."

"The setting and characters are too limited," another editor argued. "If we're going to do anything revolving around athletics, it should be another horse series."

"Talk about limited!" the first editor countered.

"What we need here," Ms. Miller broke in, a tense look on her face, "is something fresher. Stories that girls will enjoy. Characters that readers can identify with."

Ms. Miller's words sent Elizabeth's thoughts spinning. *Something girls would enjoy*, she thought. *Characters that readers can identify with.* Suddenly she had an amazing, incredible, impossibly great idea. "What about a twins series?" she blurted out, unable to contain herself.

"What was that?" Ms. Miller asked.

Every head at the conference table turned in Elizabeth's direction. Twelve pairs of eyes bored in on her, and she felt herself blushing.

"Did she say *twins*?" a redheaded woman in a green sweater asked.

"What kind of twins?" a young man in a blue blazer asked curiously.

"Just ordinary sixth-grade girls who are twins," Elizabeth said.

The redheaded woman nodded eagerly. "I think she might be on to something."

"Tell us a little bit more about these twins," Ms. Miller said.

"Well," Elizabeth began, overcoming her embarrassment and trying to sound as professional as possible, "in the series I envision, the two girls would look exactly alike. And they would be really good friends. But they would be totally different people. I mean, they would have really different personalities."

The redheaded woman sat with her pen poised to take notes. "You mean one sister would be responsible and dependable and a good student? And the other sister would be more spontaneous, adventurous, and funny?"

Elizabeth nodded. "Yes. But I wouldn't want

the responsible and studious twin to seem dull or unimaginative," she said firmly. "She would get involved in a lot of adventures herself."

Ms. Miller sat forward and clasped her hands together on the table. "Like what? Can you suggest some story lines?"

Elizabeth ran a mental review of all the fun, crazy, silly, and scary things that she and Jessica had experienced together. "Well," she said in a musing voice, "right off the top of my head, I could probably give you three or four story suggestions. . . ."

"Elizabeth, you're a genius," Ms. Miller said later, after the meeting had broken up. "I would like you to come to work for us on a full-time basis—as my executive assistant. There is a lot of responsibility attached to the job, but you seem like a very responsible young woman."

"Gee," Elizabeth said, blushing, "I hope that doesn't mean you think I'm dull."

Ms. Miller smiled. "Not at all. You're clearly both responsible and imaginative. In fact, that's one reason I want you involved in the Sweet Valley Twins book series. I think we ought to model one of the twins on your personality."

Elizabeth grinned appreciatively. "That would really be an honor."

"So will you take the job?"

"May I think about it over the weekend?" Elizabeth asked.

"Absolutely," Ms. Miller replied. "Take as much time as you need. But I do truly hope that you'll say yes. You have a lot of talent—and a big future in this business."

"Thank you," Elizabeth said proudly. As she walked back down the hall toward the front desk, she realized that she was very glad to have been a success. But for some reason she wasn't exactly elated.

In fact, she felt strange and a little sad. Homesick for something that wasn't home. She felt like a visitor in a foreign country where no one spoke her language.

It was lonely being a girl in a woman's body, and Elizabeth realized that right now, what she wanted more than anything else in the world was to be with her sister.

Nineteen

As Elizabeth hurried down the sidewalk, the heels of her blue loafers made an efficient tapping sound on the pavement. She noticed several people turning to admire her, but Elizabeth didn't feel complimented. She was tired of being looked at, and she was willing to bet that Jessica was, too.

In fact, if Jessica had been forced to cope with even half the instructions, criticisms, compliments, and information that Elizabeth had had to contend with, there was probably nothing left of her but a limp and wrung-out rag.

It's definitely tiring being an adult, she decided. *I'm just about ready to go back to being twelve. And I bet Jess won't have any big objections to that.*

Of course, she wasn't exactly sure how to get

her twelve-year-old body back, but she guessed that the logical place to start would be the wishing well at the carnival.

The thought of returning to her twelve-year-old world set off a fresh wave of yearning. She wanted to go home and see her mom and her dad. She wanted to hear Jessica running to the telephone every five minutes and Steven complaining about it. She wanted to smell her mother's Christmas baking and listen to her father's silly Christmas stories about Santa and the North Pole.

She was crying now. Tears streamed down her cheeks, and she had to stop to find a tissue. She located the cellophane package in her pocket, and immediately dried her eyes and blew her nose.

"Elizabeth!" A pair of strong arms wrapped around her waist and swung her around.

"Jessica!" Elizabeth laughed as they both practically fell over. "You can't believe how happy I am to see you."

"Yes, I can," Jessica said. "You can't believe how much I was missing you by this afternoon."

"I missed you, too," Elizabeth responded. "So how was the filing?"

"The filing didn't work out too well," Jessica said in an embarrassed voice.

"I didn't think it would," Elizabeth said with a smile, "so if you don't mind, let's—"

"But the designing worked out great!" Jessica interrupted.

Elizabeth stared at her sister. *Designing? What's she talking about?*

"You won't believe it, Lizzie," Jessica continued breathlessly. "It was just like something in the movies. There I was, a lowly file clerk with everybody in the whole place yelling at me, and then the big boss looks at some of my sketches and—ta-da!" Jessica struck a dramatic pose. "I was promoted to Assistant Design Consultant for the new spring line, which is called"—Jessica dropped her pose and grinned happily—"*The Jessica Collection!*"

"Are you serious?" Elizabeth asked with a gasp.

Jessica nodded happily. "I did really well, Elizabeth. They think I'm talented, and they say I have a great future in fashion design."

Elizabeth felt a strange pounding sensation. And it was in her chest *and* in her stomach.

"And guess who asked me out? Their fashion photographer. He's really good-looking, too. But I couldn't wait to tell you everything, so I told him I had a previous engagement. I'm sure he'll ask me out again sometime."

The thumping in her chest was pride,

Elizabeth decided as Jessica chattered happily on. She was proud of her sister for achieving so much in such a short amount of time.

But the thumping in her stomach was sorrow. Jessica was a big success in the grown-up world. She was a part of the fashion industry. She had made a grown-up male friend. And she had a fantastic time ahead of her.

It wouldn't be fair to ask her to go back to being twelve. Back to being treated like a child. Back to being left out of things.

Jessica threaded her arm through Elizabeth's and began steering her toward the restaurant. "We'll sleep in the room over the garage tonight. But we should start looking for an apartment tomorrow. Now, I know what you're thinking." She held up her hand. "You're wondering how we're going to pay for everything. Don't worry. I got a raise."

"A raise already?" Elizabeth exclaimed.

"I went from almost fired to full-time," Jessica joked. "There was no place to go but up." She tugged at Elizabeth's hand. "Let's hurry so we don't have to wait for a table. I'm starving. Aren't you?"

"Sure. You bet," Elizabeth said quickly, trying to sound cheerful. But the lump in her stomach was feeling so heavy, Elizabeth was pretty sure she wouldn't be able to eat a bite.

*   *   *

"A book series!" Jessica dropped her forkful of cheesecake in surprise. "The publishing company is actually going to use your idea for a book series?"

Elizabeth nodded proudly, her cheeks turning pink.

"I can't believe you let me talk on and on about what a big success I was today, when you were even more successful than I was."

"I wasn't more successful," Elizabeth protested. "I think designing a line of clothes is pretty spectacular."

"But creating books takes real talent," Jessica argued.

"Doesn't creating clothes take talent, too?" Elizabeth asked with a smile.

"Well sure, but . . ." Jessica broke off and forced herself to smile. "We both did well," she said quietly. *So why am I about to burst into tears?* she wondered.

The waitress appeared at their table with two plates. "Ready for your apple pie?" she asked Jessica.

Jessica nodded, grateful for the distraction. While the waitress placed Elizabeth's meat loaf, mashed potaoes, salad, and bread in front of her, Jessica took a few deep breaths and swallowed the sob that had been rising in her throat.

Being grown up was great—for grown-ups, that is. But Jessica missed her parents and the Unicorns and everything about being twelve. And she had been hoping that Elizabeth would be so tired, discouraged, and bewildered by her job that she would be ready to throw in the towel and go back to being twelve. But instead she was absolutely thriving on adulthood.

"They loved the story ideas I suggested," Elizabeth said as she lifted a forkful of potatoes to her mouth.

Jessica tried to look cheerful. "Tell me some of the ideas you talked about."

Elizabeth lowered her fork. "Mostly I just told them about some of the funny things that have happened to us," she answered. "Like the time we pretended to be psychic and . . ."

Jessica leaned forward and smiled, pretending to listen. But the story Elizabeth was telling made her feel more like crying than laughing. It was a typical Elizabeth-and-Jessica story. As usual, Jessica had shot off her big mouth and made a big mess. And as usual, Elizabeth had had to clean up.

Elizabeth has always been perfect for adulthood, Jessica realized. *So of course it makes sense that she's amazingly great at it already.*

Jessica cringed as she thought about all the times she'd relied on her sister's levelheaded thinking and her willingness to cooperate with her crazy schemes. *She's always helped me get something if I really wanted it. Well, now it's my turn to help her.* Now, as a grown-up, Elizabeth had a chance to do what she had always dreamed of doing. And Jessica wasn't going to take that away from her.

Knock, knock.

"Come in." Steven sat up on the edge of the bed where he had been miserably sprawled for the last few hours.

The door opened, and Mr. and Mrs. Wakefield stood in the doorway.

"It's dark, Steven," Mrs. Wakefield said. "Don't you think it's time to tell us where the girls are?"

"I wish I could tell you," Steven began, "but..." He trailed off helplessly and nervously wet his lips.

"But you promised the girls you wouldn't," Mr. Wakefield finished for him. "It's important to keep promises, Steven, but if the girls have run away..."

"They haven't run away," Steven said quickly, hoping to reassure them.

Mr. and Mrs. Wakefield exchanged a look. Then Mrs. Wakefield dropped her eyes, and Mr. Wakefield turned his level gaze back to Steven.

"We want to know where the girls are. Are you going to tell us?"

"I can't," Steven practically moaned. "I would if I could, but I can't."

"Fine," Mrs. Wakefield said in a hoarse voice. "You have to do what you think is right. So you'll understand that we have to do what we think is right. Steven, I forbid you to leave this room until the girls are home or you're ready to tell us what you know about their disappearance."

Mrs. Wakefield left quickly. Mr. Wakefield gave his son a long and disappointed stare before he left, too, quietly shutting the door behind him.

Steven fell back on the bed and groaned. Of all the adventures and misadventures the twins had gotten him involved in, this was the worst.

He glanced at his wristwatch and sat up. It was time to rendezvous with the twins.

He knew his parents would wait at least an hour before coming back to grill him again. That meant he could safely be gone an hour before they discovered that he was missing.

Steven went to the window and opened it. Slowly and cautiously, he stepped out onto the ledge. He grabbed the edge of the roof and steadied himself while he stepped onto a large branch of the tree that stood beside the house.

In a matter of seconds, he shinnied down the trunk, dropped to the ground, and stealthily made his way down the dark shadows of the driveway that led to the sidewalk.

He hoped the twins would be on time to meet him. That way, they would have time to go back to the carnival and unwish the wish tonight. He wasn't exactly sure how they'd feel about that, but he'd drag them there if he had to. No way did he want to go through another day like today.

Twenty

"I guess we'll have to buy a car," Jessica chattered happily after she and Elizabeth had met up with Steven on the edge of the little park a few blocks from their house. "Let's get something low and sporty."

"You get something low and sporty," Elizabeth said. "I want a Jeep."

Jessica nodded approvingly. "That would be cool, Lizzie. Hey, maybe we'll let Steven drive it when he gets a little older."

The twins giggled, and Steven did his best to smile. But he had never felt less like smiling in his whole life.

His sisters had grown up. Grown up in a day and left him way behind.

They've had a totally amazing day, he thought.

*How could I drag them back to childhood now?
Especially since I'm the one who made them miserable
being twelve.*

No, they definitely wouldn't want to go back
to being his little sisters. Not when they could
make lots of money, have great cars, live in an
apartment, and never have to listen to their parents again.

"Listen!" Jessica said suddenly.

"Somebody's singing," Elizabeth said, cocking
her head. "It's a choir."

Down at the end of the block, a group of kids
were gathered in the light of a streetlamp.

"Hey, that's right," Steven said. "A bunch of
kids at the party said they were planning to go
caroling tonight."

"Gee," Jessica said in a small voice. "How
come nobody invited us?"

"How could they invite us when we don't
even exist anymore?" Elizabeth shot back.

Steven was startled by the sharp edge in
Elizabeth's voice. She sounded as if she was
upset or something.

"Are you mad about something?" Jessica asked.

"No," Elizabeth said in a clipped tone.

"Well, you sounded mad."

Steven studied Elizabeth's face. The corners of
her mouth were curved upward, but somehow it
didn't look like a smile.

"I guess I'm just a little sad about not being able to carol with the gang," Elizabeth said.

"Get back," Steven warned. "Here they come.

The girls and Steven stepped back into the shadows of a large hedge as the group approached. Janet and Joe Howell were there, Lila Fowler, Todd Wilkins, Andy and Melissa McCormick, and lots of their other friends. They were bundled in sweaters and bathed in the soft glow of the streetlights.

Steven swallowed hard, trying to dislodge the lump in his throat. Elizabeth's remark made him feel awful. Every year she and Jessica insisted on singing their own, harmonized version of "Jingle Bells." And every year, they just got worse and worse. They were so bad that one year their new neighbors complained to their father that the family's cats were making too much noise.

But we don't have any cats, their bewildered father had said.

Steven involuntarily snorted with laughter as the familiar group of carolers passed by them, Amy Sutton and Maria Slater bringing up the rear.

"What's so funny?" Jessica whispered.

But before he could answer, Elizabeth stepped forward and into the light that illuminated the sidewalk. "Amy!" she exclaimed.

*   *   *

Amy stared at her with large curious eyes. "Yes?"

Elizabeth knew that what she was doing was insane. But she couldn't help it. The pain of losing Amy's friendship had suddenly seemed unbearable. She had to talk to her one last time.

"Do I know you?" Amy asked, looking a little nervous.

Elizabeth opened her mouth to speak, but no words came out. What could she say? As she stared in silence, Amy shifted uneasily and took a step backward.

"Amy, don't be afraid," Elizabeth begged, blurting out the words before she had time to think. "It's me."

Amy frowned. "I don't know who you are." Her body tensed as she prepared to run. "I—I better go."

"Amy! Please!"

But Amy turned and ran, disappearing around the hedge to catch up with the others.

"Are you crazy?" Jessica hissed as she stepped out and grabbed Elizabeth's arm.

"I'm sorry. I'm sorry," Elizabeth whispered, trying hard not to choke.

"Come on," Steven said nervously. "Let's cut across Elm. That way if anybody comes back to investigate, we'll be long gone."

Elizabeth nodded, and the three of them

jogged across the pavement, hurried through an alley, and emerged on the west side of Elm, where the overhanging tree branches kept the pavement in shadow.

As they made their way down the street, Elizabeth was grateful for the dark. She didn't want Jessica or Steven to see her tears and notice how upset she was. It would spoil their good mood.

". . . the problem with those cars is that they're hard to fix and you have to wait a long time for parts," Steven was saying.

"Yeah. But just think what a great beach car it would be," Jessica responded. "Think about it, Steven. You'll get your learner's permit when you're fifteen. That means you can drive with an adult. And guess who's an adult now?"

Jessica and Steven began planning all the great road trips the three of them would take. By the time the Wakefields' house came into view, they had been to Aspen, New York, Seattle, and Miami Beach.

"Shhh," Steven warned when they reached the edge of the lawn. "Once we go up the driveway," he instructed, "make a straight line toward the garage and stay in the shadows."

Twenty-one

"Smells musty," Jessica whispered as they quietly made their way up the stairs.

Elizabeth couldn't comment, because the familiar smell of the garage had brought another lump to her throat. *I can't believe I'm getting all emotional about the smell of cars, bags of junk, piles of newspapers, and stacks of cardboard boxes.*

But it wasn't just the smell of a garage, it was the smell of her childhood. It was the smell of bicycles and balls and croquet mallets and the old clothes that were kept in the dress-up trunk.

The steps creaked and groaned as the three of them made their way to the room upstairs. But no one said a word until they had entered the room and closed the door behind them.

"The shades are down," Steven said. "But

don't turn on any lights until they go up to bed, OK? Otherwise, they might see the light through the crack."

"OK," Jessica agreed.

"Make sure Jessica doesn't forget," he said to Elizabeth.

"Hey!" Jessica teased. "Quit talking about me like I'm an irresponsible kid. I happen to be the Assistant Design Consultant at Y and C Clothing, Inc."

"It's *important*, Jessica," Steven insisted in an angry voice. "If Mom and Dad see the light, they'll come and investigate. They might even call the police, and then what am I supposed to do?"

"Chill out, Steven, will you?" Jessica said. "Why are you getting so mad all of a sudden?"

"I'm not mad," Steven said in a mad voice. "I'm just trying to keep things from getting totally out of hand."

"*You're* trying to keep things from getting totally out of hand," Jessica repeated in insulted surprise. "Who put you in charge?"

"Nature," he snapped. "I'm the oldest."

"Not anymore, pal," Jessica said angrily. "If you don't believe me, look in the mirror."

"Shut up," Elizabeth practically shouted. "Both of you shut up right now!"

She could see Steven's and Jessica's amazed faces in the tiny crack of moonlight that poured

in over the shade. She knew it was rare that anyone heard her lose her temper. Both their jaws fell
open in surprise.

"What's wrong, Elizabeth?" Jessica finally
said.

Elizabeth turned her to the window and
pulled the shade open a bit so that she could see
the house. What would happen if she did what
she most wanted to do? If she ran down the stairs
and burst into the house shouting, "Mom! Dad!"
Would they ever believe that she was really
Elizabeth? Would they open their arms and wel-
come her home? Or would they scream and call
the police?

"Elizabeth?" Steven prompted.

Elizabeth didn't answer. She knew that if she
tried to speak she'd only start sobbing.

"What are you looking at?" Jessica whispered.

Steven and Jessica stood at Elizabeth's elbow
and peered at the house.

As they watched, a light suddenly came on in
Elizabeth's room. She gasped and leaned closer,
pressing her nose to the window. Through the
bedroom window, she could see her parents
standing in her doorway. They stood motionless
for a few moments as their eyes swept the room.
Elizabeth had never seen them look so sad. Then
Mr. Wakefield's hand lifted toward the light
switch, and the room was dark again.

"What are they doing in our rooms?" Jessica asked as the lights in her bedroom went on.

"Hoping against hope that they'll find us there, I guess," Elizabeth said softly.

Mr. and Mrs. Wakefield looked around Jessica's room. Then Mrs. Wakefield went to the window. Elizabeth felt the strangest sensation. Her mother was looking straight at the garage window. Straight at Elizabeth. But it was dark, and Elizabeth knew that her mother had no idea that she was being watched.

"Tonight was the night we were supposed to go get our Christmas tree," Elizabeth said softly, hearing a little wobble in her voice.

As they watched, Mrs. Wakefield's face crumpled, and her shoulders began to shake. Mr. Wakefield quickly came up behind her and put his hands on her shoulders, trying to comfort her.

They exchanged a few words, and Mrs. Wakefield nodded. Mr. Wakefield took Mrs. Wakefield's hand and led her from the room, pausing only to tap the light switch, plunging the room back into darkness.

"That does it!" Steven practically shouted. "You two are the most selfish people on the whole planet."

"Me? Selfish?" Elizabeth and Jessica exclaimed at once, whirling to face Steven.

He folded his arms. "Yeah. Selfish. Just because you guys are grown-ups and have really great jobs and everything, you're going to run out on Mom and Dad and never look back. Did either one of you stop to think how I—I mean *they*—would feel? Don't you think that I—that *they* would miss you? Don't you think I—I mean . . ." Steven made an impatient gesture with his shoulders. "OK. I mean me. Didn't you ever stop to wonder how I would feel?"

"We know how you feel," Jessica retorted.

"That's right," Elizabeth said. "You made it pretty clear. *Nothing's the matter with me except that I'm going to have two sisters at Joe Howell's party that are going to totally embarrass me.*" She lowered her voice to imitate Steven.

Steven's face softened. "Ohhh, Lizzie, I didn't mean that."

"Or this one: *Don't come to Joe's party. Please. I'll do your chores for two weeks?*"

Steven hung his head. "I'm sorry. I take it all back."

"You can't take it back," Jessica fumed. "The party's already over, and I didn't see you trying to convince Mom and Dad to let us go."

"OK. I was wrong. I was stupid. I was mean. For whatever it's worth now, I'm sorry. But if you won't do it for me, do it for Mom and Dad."

"Do what?" Elizabeth asked evenly.

"Come back home. Go back to being twelve."

"I thought you were looking forward to being able to drive with your two older sisters," Elizabeth said tightly.

Steven shook his head. "I just said that because you two seemed so happy and excited about everything. I didn't feel like I had any right to ask you guys to give it all up. I was trying not to be selfish."

Elizabeth looked at her sister. "Jess?" she said quietly, hopefully.

Jessica looked at her, a serious expression on her face. "I'll go back if you want to go back."

"But what do *you* want?" Elizabeth pressed. She held her breath.

"I do want to go back," Jessica said quietly. "But I don't want you to have to give up the job of your dreams. If you want to be a grown-up, I'll be a grown-up with you. And if you want to be a twelve-year-old again, I'll be a twelve-year-old with you. I'm your twin. So wherever you go, I'm going, too."

Elizabeth was truly touched. It wasn't often that Jessica put Elizabeth's feelings before her own. "I do want to go back," she admitted. "But just like you, I didn't want to drag you along with me and make you miss out on something wonderful."

Steven chuckled. "Boy. For three selfish people, we sure have been doing a lot of self-sacrificing."

Elizabeth put an arm around her siblings and squeezed their shoulders. "Then it's unanimous. Jess and I will go back to being twelve again."

"How?" Jessica asked.

Elizabeth shrugged. "I guess we get out of this fix the same way we got into it."

"Think Mom and Dad will go into your room to look for you?" Elizabeth asked Steven on the walk to the carnival.

Steven nodded. "Probably. They'll hit the ceiling when they realize I snuck out. But I figure if I come back home with two twelve-year-old twins, they'll forgive and forget."

"What if it doesn't work?" Elizabeth said in a worried voice.

"It'll work," Steven said confidently. "It worked before, why shouldn't it work again? Jessica, come *on*. You've been half a block behind us ever since we left the house."

"I can't help it," Jessica moaned. "These shoes are killing me. I'll bet I walked a thousand miles today."

"Only two more blocks," Steven said in an encouraging tone.

"That's what you said two blocks ago," Jessica pointed out.

"Yeah, but this time it's true," Steven promised.

Elizabeth giggled.

"Don't encourage him," Jessica warned. But she couldn't help smiling herself. As they got closer and closer to the Christmas carnival, things between the three of them seemed to be getting more and more normal. Steven was teasing, and Elizabeth was giggling, and Jessica was complaining. Ordinary as it was, there was no place like home. Jessica couldn't wait to wish her way out of this grown-up business and get back to her own life, her own wardrobe, and her own bed.

"Boy, am I glad I don't have to go back to work on Monday," she said with a laugh. "Make that—Boy am I glad I don't have to go back to work, ever."

"You'll have to go to work someday," Steven corrected in a teasing tone.

"Right," Jessica agreed. "But not for a long time. I've got a few other things I want to do first."

"Such as?"

"Such as getting a good night's sleep in my own bed. Eating lots of Dad's special pancakes. Going to Unicorn meetings, and . . ." Jessica noticed that Elizabeth and Steven had gotten ahead of her again. Maybe she would be better off barefoot. She stopped and bent down to remove her shoes.

"I'm glad I don't have to go to work on Monday, too," she heard Elizabeth say as she and Steven disappeared around the corner. "If I had to go back tomorrow, I think I would . . ." Her voice broke off with a cry of alarm.

"Hey!" Steven shouted hoarsely, and Jessica felt a chill run up her spine. She kicked off her shoes and jogged around the corner to catch up. When she did, her mouth fell open and her heart plummeted right down into her bare feet. She couldn't believe it. She couldn't believe it at all.

"The Christmas carnival!" she cried. "It's gone!"

Twenty-two

Jessica wandered around in a big circle, moodily kicking at the tin cans, scraps of paper, and popped balloons that littered the fairgrounds.

"I can't believe it," Steven said for about the fifteenth time. His face had gone white with shock.

"What are we going to do, Jess?" Elizabeth whispered.

Jessica swallowed hard, unable to answer.

Two city trash trucks rumbled up the road and pulled to a stop with a loud whoosh and roar. Three men jumped out of each truck carrying long brooms.

"If you're looking for the Christmas carnival," one of them said, "you're too late."

"Where did it go?" Jessica asked.

"I think their next stop was supposed to be Littlefield," one of the men said.

"That's three hours away," Steven said unhappily.

"More like four," one of the other men commented. "Unless you take the express bus. Then it's three and a half."

"There's a bus?" all three said at the same time.

One of the men pointed. "That way. About two blocks. It leaves every half hour."

Jessica broke into a run, ignoring the pain in her feet. "Come on," she urged the other two. "The sooner we get to Littlefield, the sooner we'll be back to normal."

"This is it?" Elizabeth asked as the bus stopped.

The bus driver nodded. "This is it. The Littlefield fairgrounds."

"But it's so dark," Jessica commented.

"Yeah!" Steven agreed. "Where are all the people?"

The bus driver shrugged. "Beats me. You want to get off or not?"

Elizabeth nodded. "We're getting off. Come on, Jess. Come on, Steven."

The minute they stepped off the bus, the door closed behind them, and the bus roared off into the night.

"This is really spooky," Jessica said.

Elizabeth looked all around. The carnival was set up. But there wasn't a soul around. It was desolate and shrouded in darkness. It really was spooky.

A car came cruising up the street and slowed down as it passed Elizabeth and Jessica. A man's face peered out of the window on the passenger side.

Steven bristled and protectively stepped in front of his sisters. "What are you looking at?" he yelled at the car.

The car immediately sped up and drove off.

"Come on," Steven said. "The gate's over there. Maybe they'll have a sign or something telling us when they open."

Elizabeth followed Jessica and Steven over to the gate. But there was no sign up and nobody in sight to ask.

Steven shook the chain on the gate in frustration. "Hello!" he called out. "Hello!"

"Go away," a high-pitched voice in the dark instructed.

Elizabeth jumped, and so did Steven and Jessica.

"We don't officially open until tomorrow," the voice said.

"But we need to come in tonight," Jessica wailed.

An overhead light suddenly switched on and bathed the three of them in warm yellow light.

"You're too old for the Christmas carnival," the voice argued. "The Christmas carnival is for kids."

"We are kids," Elizabeth insisted. "Or at least we were until we made a wish at the wishing well."

Suddenly, two elfin people appeared out of the shadows—a small man and a small woman.

"I know you," Jessica said to the lady in a voice full of amazement. "You're the lady who sold me the clothes."

"And you're the chestnut vendor," Elizabeth exclaimed to the man. "Remember us? You wished us an unforgettable Christmas."

The chestnut vendor and the woman stood silently, smiling at the group with twinkling eyes.

"Can't we just come in and make a wish?" Elizabeth begged. "It won't take long and . . . and . . . if we can't make our wish, this will be the most miserable Christmas of our whole lives."

"Well, why didn't you say so?" the elfin man said. He lifted his hand, and the gate seemed to swing open magically.

Elizabeth led the way inside. The minute they stepped through the gate, she gasped. Every single light in the carnival had come on, and the place glittered and blazed.

There were white lights, green lights, red lights, and gold lights. Everywhere she looked, Christmas trees shimmered and glittered, and Christmas music filled the air.

Elizabeth turned to thank the elfin couple, but they had vanished.

"Come on," Jessica said, tugging on her arm. "I think the wishing well is this way."

Elizabeth ran with Jessica and Steven through the carnival—past the Ferris wheel, past the tunnel of love, and past the merry-go-round.

"There it is!" Steven cried.

The three of them gathered at the well, panting for breath.

"OK," Steven said. "Who's first?"

Elizabeth dug her hand into her pocket. "Uh-oh, I don't have a coin."

Jessica's face looked stricken, and she frantically searched her own pockets. "Neither do I."

Steven thrust his hand down into the pocket of his jacket and retrieved one quarter. "This is it," he said in a gloomy voice.

"Think it'll work with three on a wish?" Jessica asked fearfully.

Elizabeth shook her head. "I don't know. All we can do is try."

Steven held the coin out over the well, and all three of them pinched a tiny portion of the coin's edge.

"Close your eyes," Jessica instructed.

Elizabeth closed her eyes as tightly as she could.

"Now wish!" Jessica instructed.

I wish I were twelve again, Elizabeth wished. *And I wish Jessica were twelve again, too.*

All three let go and . . .

Plink!

Elizabeth opened her eyes, and as soon as she did, she was almost sick with disappointment.

Jessica was still grown up, and so was she.

"It didn't work," Elizabeth whispered sadly, feeling warm tears fill her eyes.

"Don't give up yet," Jessica pleaded in a broken voice.

"Come on," Steven said nervously. "Let's get out of here."

Elizabeth didn't wait. She turned and began running back toward the entrance as fast as she could.

The place seemed hideous and frightening now. And over the sound of Christmas music, she could hear the sound of someone laughing.

"Sweet Valley," the bus driver called.

Steven stared gloomily out the window.

"Hey! Son! This is Sweet Valley."

Steven jumped when he realized the driver was speaking to him. And when he looked out the window, he recognized the Sweet Valley bus stop.

They were home.

The twins had lain down across seats in the back of the bus to sleep. But Steven had been too nervous to sleep. He'd been trying to think of what he would tell his parents. Not only would he be up a creek for sneaking out, he wouldn't be able to explain what had happened to Elizabeth and Jessica.

Steven imagined his parents' anger and frustration with him. They might even wind up calling the police in to talk the truth out of him.

He swallowed hard. He had a horrible knot in his stomach, and he was close to tears. *We went all this way, and we're just as bad off as we were yesterday,* he thought. *Actually, we're worse off,* he amended. *Because now we're broke.*

"Hate to hurry you, son. But I've got to turn this bus in."

Steven nodded and turned in his seat. "Jessica! Elizabeth!" he called out.

There was a loud yawn from the back of the bus, and a tousled blond head popped up and into view.

One second later, a second tousled blond head popped up.

Steven's eyes widened, and his eyebrows shot up. He almost jumped through the roof of the bus, he was so overjoyed.

Those tousled blond heads belonged to two very tired, very rumpled twelve-year-old twins.

"That's strange," the bus driver said, scratching his head in perplexity. "I could have sworn you got on this bus with two women."

Steven began to laugh. He was laughing so hard that tears were rolling down his cheeks. It was the first really good laugh he had had in a long time.

"Dad! Dad!"

Mr. Wakefield was still dressed in the clothes he had been wearing the day before as he stooped wearily over to pick up the morning paper.

"Dad!" the twins and Steven cried again as they came running up the street.

Suddenly Mr. Wakefield looked up. His face filled with joy and relief. "Elizabeth!" he shouted. "Jessica!" He dropped the paper and ran toward the girls with open arms. "Alice!" he shouted. "Alice! They're home!"

Just as Mr. Wakefield's arms closed around Elizabeth and Jessica, their mother came flying out the front door and across the lawn. Tears were streaming down her cheeks. "You're home," she murmured through her tears. "Oh, thank heavens you're home."

Elizabeth felt tears streaming down her own cheeks. Seeing the weary slump of her father's shoulders and her mother's red and swollen eyes made her realize just how horrendous the last twenty-four hours had been for them. "I'm sorry," she choked. "I'm so sorry. It's really hard to explain what happened—" she began.

But her father cut her off. "I don't care what happened," he said in a voice thick with emotion. "I don't even want to hear it. You're all grounded until after Christmas." He held up his hand, as if to ward off objections. "That means you're sentenced to a solid week and a half of tree decorating, cookie baking, carol singing, present opening, and worst of all—a solid week and a half of being together."

They all began to laugh.

"If that's what I have to do to have an old-fashioned Christmas," Mr. Wakefield said, hugging the girls even tighter, "then that's what I'm going to do. Any complaints?"

"Not from me," Steven said with a smile.

"Me either," Elizabeth said.

Jessica thought about it for a few moments, then she grinned. "I've never been so happy to be grounded. In fact, I think it's going to be the happiest *and* most unforgettable Christmas of my whole life."

SIGN UP FOR THE SWEET VALLEY HIGH® FAN CLUB!

Hey, girls! Get all the gossip on Sweet Valley High's® most popular teenagers when you join our fantastic Fan Club! As a member, you'll get all of this really cool stuff:

- Membership Card with your own personal Fan Club ID number
- A Sweet Valley High® Secret Treasure Box
- Sweet Valley High® Stationery
- Official Fan Club Pencil (for secret note writing!)
- Three Bookmarks
- A "Members Only" Door Hanger
- Two Skeins of J. & P. Coats® Embroidery Floss with flower barrette instruction leaflet
- Two editions of *The Oracle* newsletter
- Plus exclusive Sweet Valley High® product offers, special savings, contests, and much more!

Be the first to find out what Jessica & Elizabeth Wakefield are up to by joining the Sweet Valley High® Fan Club for the one-year membership fee of only $6.25 each for U.S. residents, $8.25 for Canadian residents (U.S. currency). Includes shipping & handling.

Send a check or money order (do not send cash) made payable to "Sweet Valley High® Fan Club" along with this form to:

SWEET VALLEY HIGH® FAN CLUB, BOX 3919-B, SCHAUMBURG, IL 60168-3919

NAME_____
(Please print clearly)

ADDRESS_____

CITY_____ STATE _____ ZIP_____
(Required)

AGE _____ BIRTHDAY_____ /_____ /_____

Offer good while supplies last. Allow 6-8 weeks after check clearance for delivery. Addresses without ZIP codes cannot be honored. Offer good in USA & Canada only. Void where prohibited by law.
©1993 by Francine Pascal   LCI-1383-123